THE
PRINCE WHO FELL
FROM THE SKY

ALSO BY JOHN CLAUDE BEMIS

THE CLOCKWORK DARK

The Nine Pound Hammer
The Wolf Tree
The White City

The PRINCE WHO FELL from the SKY

JOHN CLAUDE BEMIS

Random House 🏠 New York

All rights reserved. Published in the United States by Random House Children's Books, a division of Random House, Inc., New York.

Random House and the colophon are registered trademarks of Random House, Inc.

Visit us on the Web! randomhouse.com/kids

Educators and librarians, for a variety of teaching tools, visit us at randomhouse.com/teachers

Library of Congress Cataloging-in-Publication Data
Bemis, John Claude.
The prince who fell from the sky / John Claude Bemis. — 1st ed.
p. cm.
Summary: When an orbital spacecraft crashes on a post-apocalyptic Earth where animals have regained control, a cubless mother bear adopts the lone survivor, a young boy, and leads him on a journey toward safety from the ruling wolf clans.
ISBN 978-0-375-86752-1 (trade) — ISBN 978-0-375-96752-8 (lib. bdg.) —
ISBN 978-0-375-89804-4 (ebook)
[1. Human-animal relationships—Fiction. 2. Bears—Fiction. 3. Wolves—Fiction. 4. Animals—Fiction. 5. Forests and forestry—Fiction. 6. Voyages and travels—Fiction.] I. Title.
PZ7.B4237Pri 2012 [Fic]—dc23 2011020509

Printed in the United States of America

10 9 8 7 6 5 4 3 2 1

First Edition

For Rose

THE
PRINCE WHO FELL
FROM THE SKY

CHAPTER ONE

The Forest was green with summer when the bear lumbered up from the creek bed where she had been cooling off. As she crested the bank, she paused to sniff. The air was heavy with the scent of new life.

Moist smells. Earthy smells. Flowery smells.

And mixed with them was the sweet aroma of death.

The bear's coppery-black body was massive, and it was nothing for her to push aside saplings and tangles of creeper as she followed her nose toward the carcass.

The odor grew ripe. She hurried, loping through a bed of the relics rusting among the laurels. She drew in a deep sniff and stopped.

She had found it. But she was not alone.

She edged out from the thicket of laurels. A trio of cubs tumbled on the ground. At the sight of Casseomae, they squealed and ran clumsily toward their mother, who was eating from a day-old elk, her face buried in the cavity of the elk's body. She lifted her face at the sound of her cubs. Blood was smeared on her snout and nose. An assembly of crows who were waiting for their turn in the branches of a hickory overhead began jeering with loud caws.

The sow rose and circled around from behind the carcass. "Get behind me, cubs," she growled, and they retreated nervously behind their mother. "You know you are not welcome, Casseomae. I've warned you before."

"I don't mean harm," Casseomae said, dipping her head. "Not to you, Dubhe, or to your cubs. I only thought we might share this—"

Dubhe bounced on stiff front legs and popped her jaws, as their kind would to show menace. "And let you curse my cubs! No, get away from here, witch, before you steal their breath away like you did your own—"

"That's enough, Dubhe!"

Dubhe dipped her nose to the newcomer. "Alioth!"

Dubhe's cubs dropped to their bellies at the sight of their chief. "Big One," they whimpered in unison.

Alioth lumbered forward slowly, his fur looking almost red as he passed through a patch of sunlight. He was not the biggest of their clan, but he had been tough enough and strong enough to convince even the larger

2

males that he was their chief. He was the Big One and had been for several summers now.

"Dubhe," Alioth grumbled as he came closer. "What have I said about that sort of talk? Let us all finish this lucky find together. And with haste before the Ogeema's hunters smell it."

Alioth shuffled over to the elk and bit in greedily, but neither Casseomae nor Dubhe moved. The chief pulled a stretchy piece of tissue and crunched, looking back at the sows.

"Come now," he said. "Don't let grudges dampen your appetites."

Dubhe nudged her cubs to leave. Quickly Casseomae said, "No, let Dubhe share the viand with you, Big One. She has cubs to feed. I'll forage. The Forest is rich. Isn't that what we old sows always say?"

Casseomae trotted off through the trees. She hadn't gotten far before Alioth called out behind her, "Casseomae." When he caught up, the bear chief spoke in a low voice. "You're still mourning. What can I do for you?"

"Nothing, Big One," she replied.

"Don't call me that, Casseomae. You of all my bears don't have to call me that."

She gave a huff. "I'm fine, Alioth. Don't worry about me."

"But I do," the chief said. "I always have."

She bowed her head and turned to go back to her meadow. Alioth called out, "The bear's path is marked by heavy steps. You remember, don't you? You taught me that lesson long ago."

"I remember, Alioth," she said, and lumbered away.

CHAPTER TWO

Casseomae reached the meadow with the sun high overhead. The air was still and hot, buzzing with insects. Casseomae spent most of her time here. It was her meadow, as much as anything can belong to a bear. It abounded for much of the year with fruit and flowers and tasty shoots. She had hunted and foraged here her whole life. Just over on the far side, beyond the rows of vine-covered relics, was the little den of wood and stone where she had given birth to several litters of stillborn cubs.

Snapping a grasshopper from a milkweed stalk, she climbed onto the nearest of the relics. Its dilapidated frame creaked under her weight. Normally bears and bigger vora hunters found it unwise to climb on the relics of the Skinless Ones. Tangled in fox grape and honeysuckle, the hulking metal shells could easily pass as shrubs, but the vines masked sharp edges of rusted metal and pits of jagged glass.

Casseomae had learned how to maneuver these dangers. She'd plopped down on the top to enjoy the sun when she heard the yaps of coyotes nearing. They'll go around, she thought. Voras almost never entered her meadow. Even the Ogeema's guard, whom she could never have denied access, always avoided her meadow. But the cries grew louder.

Casseomae sat up and shook out her mane. Coyotes posed no threat to a bear of her size. She could drive them away without a fight. But today, with Dubhe's words still stinging, she wouldn't have minded a fight.

The yapping grew until at last five coyotes, one after the other, burst through the brush into the bright sun of the clearing. Something small—some little viand, a rodent maybe—dashed through the tall grass and sumac in front of the pack. It had a strange scent about it— acrid and heavily laden with the odor of Skinless relics.

The coyotes circled one of the vine-covered dilapidations, digging at the edges of its frame. "It's under here, routs!" one called to the others. "Watch that other side that it doesn't escape!"

As the coyotes dug and barked and ran around, Casseomae saw the creature emerge through the vines at the top of the relic. It was a rat, just a little brown

6

blur of fur. The creature ran to the edge of the relic and leaped to the next, and then to the next. It was halfway to Casseomae before one of the coyotes caught its scent. "It's getting away!"

"You can sniff it, you sons of curs!" the rat called back to them. "You won't catch Dumpster. Ri-ee! Ri-ee! Go lick your unders, you cur lovers, you Old Devil slaves!"

Casseomae reared up in surprise. The rat was speaking in Vorago, the common tongue used by all the vora hunters. How could a rat speak Vorago? None of the viands spoke Vorago.

The coyotes tore around the relics in a rage to catch the little creature. For all his tough talk, the rat was nearing the last of the rusting relics before an open section of field with nowhere to hide. Casseomae was almost disappointed that such a brave viand would meet its end at the jaws of the most vile of all voras, the coyotes. But such was the way of the Forest—voras hunted viands.

The rat landed on top of the last relic and scampered in a circle, searching for an escape. The coyotes surrounded below. The biggest, a female named Rend whom Casseomae had encountered before, said, "Nowhere to go now, loudmouth! We've got you."

The rat was big for his kind, nearly the size of a squirrel. Casseomae had eaten a few plump marsh rats in her time, but this creature was muscular, with a long powerful tail. He wouldn't taste very good, she decided. Especially if he talked.

"You've not got me yet, you dung-heads," the rat said, twitching his whiskers as he peered down at the circling coyotes. "You know what you got? You mess with Dumpster and you've got spittin' trouble. Nothing but spittin' trouble!"

Rend leaped onto the flat front of the relic. "I don't think so," she snarled, exposing her shimmering teeth. She inched toward the honeysuckle-covered slope leading to the top.

"Come on up here, whelp," the rat spat, backing to the far side of the relic's top. "You put just one spittin' paw on this car and I'll send you scurrying back to your hound of a mother!"

"You won't talk so brave from the bottom of my stomach," Rend growled as she leaped for the creature.

In the fraction of a moment before Rend's paws met the vine-tangled slope, Casseomae realized what the little rat had done. This Dumpster was smart. He'd provoked the coyote into a trap. What appeared to be a solid slope was in fact a thin veil of honeysuckle over a pit of jagged glass.

Rend's front paws punched through the vines, and she disappeared with a yelp. The other coyotes backed away from the relic, not knowing what had taken their leader. Two of them tucked their tails and raced away into the trees.

Dumpster reached into the shattered slope and plucked out a sliver of broken glass with his teeth. Then he ran to the edge, leaped into the air, and landed in the grass with a thump.

As Rend fought to escape, she howled, "Don't let him get away!"

The little rat was headed for Casseomae's relic, but he was too far away. With a leap, the two remaining coyotes were on him. There was a rustle of commotion in the grass and then the coyotes yipped in pain, one after the other drawing back. Blood ran freely from slashes along their snouts.

With a final dash, Dumpster squeezed under the bear's relic. Casseomae dropped down from the top and stood in front of the coyotes.

"Let us pass, old sow!" one of them barked.

The bear struck the earth with her paw, raking her long claws through the grass. "When did I start taking orders from coyotes?"

The two edged side to side, their tongues dangling, their yellow eyes looking up warily. "That creature is ours by law. He's one of the Faithful."

Dumpster cried out, "Liars! Call me that again and I'll slice your tongues from your muzzles."

Casseomae glanced over her shoulder. Dumpster

gazed out from beneath the relic, his black eyes flickering from one coyote to the other and his tail lashing back and forth.

"A Faithful? He doesn't look like a cur to me," Casseomae said to the coyotes.

Rend climbed out of the pit of glass and leaped down, her breast and front legs bloody. Limping forward, the coyote said, "Not all that served the Skinless were curs."

Casseomae snorted. "I didn't know his kind served the Skinless Ones."

Dumpster shouted, "We didn't!" at the same time Rend barked, "They did!" Rend quickly added, "His clan lives in the Skinless's cities, don't they? Clinging to the nests of their former masters. Wishing they would come back—"

"You lying pile of puke!" Dumpster shrieked.

"This isn't the first time we've caught the scent of his sort coming down the stone trails from the city," Rend said. "Others of his kind have been sneaking into the Forest, defying the Ogeema's orders."

"All this nonsense about the Faithful," Casseomae grunted. "Would you catch a bird that's nested in the ruins of a Skinless's den and call it a Faithful? You must be desperate to win the Ogeema's favor again, Rend."

Rend growled. "I'm telling you that rat is one of the Faithful. And if you don't step aside, Casseomae, you'll answer to Ogeema Dire and his wolves next."

The she-bear distended her lips and struck the ground. The coyotes scurried back a few paces. "I don't answer to dogs!" Casseomae growled.

"You're reckless, old bear," barked Rend. "You always have been. You're making a terrible mistake crossing Ogeema Dire—"

Casseomae lunged forward on stiff front legs, roaring as if to shake the earth. And for a moment, she thought she had. A boom resounded from overhead. Over the tree line, a ball of flames appeared against the blue sky. Then it was gone. In its place hovered a small shadow.

Casseomae rose on her hind legs, trying to make sense of it with her nose and her ears. Whatever it was, it was rapidly growing larger. She looked down at the coyotes, who were watching with wide yellow eyes. The rat, too, had come out from beneath the underbelly of the relic to stare at the growing shape.

"What is it?" one of the coyotes whined.

"I don't know," Rend said. "A bird?"

The shadow was taking shape now. It looked to Casseomae like an enormous insect—shiny and armored and sailing on wide wings. Lines of mist or possibly smoke trailed behind it. A cry emanated from the object, shrill and growing louder as the flying thing got closer.

"That's no bird, you idiots," the rat said.

"Then what is it?" Casseomae asked. The noise was so loud, she had to roar to be heard.

When she got no answer, she turned. The rat was gone. Tails tucked, the coyotes were dashing for the tree line. The ground began to vibrate. Casseomae dropped to her front paws as the sky darkened.

With a deafening roar, the object sailed over the meadow. Casseomae could see the entire underbelly of the thing, but it made no sense to her. It could not have been an insect or any other creature of the Forest. Nor was it a storm cloud or anything else she had ever seen sent down by the sky. In some ways it reminded her of the relics that littered the Forest, but this was much bigger and it wasn't rusted and crumbling. Casseomae saw white flames spitting from the rear of the object as it disappeared over the treetops.

Then she heard tree trunks splintering and snapping. The earth shook. And a cloud of brown dust burst into the sky.

Whatever the thing was, it had just fallen to the Forest.

CHAPTER THREE

The bear had never experienced anything to compare with what she had just seen. She had hunkered down in dirt caves and in the ancient dens of Skinless Ones during many terrible storms of ice and thunder and tornado winds. But her instincts had always forewarned her.

This had come with no warning.

As clouds of dust drifted over her glade, a family of deer broke from the trees. Other animals too were running from the thing that had crashed in the Forest—squirrels and foxes, raccoons and woodchucks. They cried out to one another in their viand languages. Birds of all sorts flocked together over the treetops as they flew away.

Casseomae understood their urge. They could not

help themselves. But she was different. She was a bear, and while the Ogeema and his wolves might rule over her sloth, there was nothing left in the Forest that hunted her kind. Her instincts told her to go forward to see what this thing was.

Casseomae went into the trees and soon saw that the dense canopy of leaves above had been torn open. A huge scar cut through the Forest flooded it with sunlight. Oaks, beeches, and hickories lay knocked aside as if they'd been little more than saplings.

She crested a hill and saw it. The thing's nose was half-buried in earth with crumpled trees piled around its front. Casseomae rose to her hind legs and sniffed. The odors stung her nose and made her eyes drip and her tongue numb. She snorted and dropped back to the ground, gazing from one end of the thing to the other.

She heard a scampering in the leaves behind her and turned. The rat stopped with one paw raised, his bulging black eyes on her. "It's a passering, isn't it?" he said.

"A what?" Casseomae asked, turning back to gaze at it.

The rat took quick steps, moving in little bursts of speed and then freezing to sniff and listen. He leaped onto a log and sat back on his haunches to study the thing below.

"You know," the rat said, impatient with excitement. "A starship."

"A fallen star?" she asked.

"No. A sort of vehicle, like those rusting cars back in your meadow. An Old Devil relic."

"Old Devils," Casseomae said. "You mean the Skinless?"

"Right. That's what you call them here in the Forest, isn't it? The Skinless Ones?"

Casseomae grunted. She knew of the Skinless Ones. Everyone knew of the Skinless Ones, even if they were long gone.

Dumpster twitched his whiskers at her. "They weren't skinless, you know."

"Then why did they hunt us?" Casseomae said. "They needed our hides because they didn't even have any skin—not any of their own. Only raw flesh and bloody tissue is what I always heard."

"How do big voras like you wind up with such tiny brains?" Dumpster said. "They might have torn the hides off us, but it wasn't because they didn't have skin of their own."

"How would you know, rat?" Casseomae said.

The rat clicked his incisors. "Because my da told me! He was the Memory for our mischief, before he passed it on to me. He knew all about the spittin' Old Devils. We rats take great pride in knowing history."

Casseomae snorted. "None of that explains why that star-relic thing landed in the Forest."

"Well, let's go find out," the rat said. He jumped from the log and scampered ahead.

"Where are you going?" Casseomae asked.

"A passering like that is probably loaded with Old Devil treasures," said the rat. "Devices. Memories. All sorts of things my mischief could use. Be back in a chirp."

Casseomae followed as Dumpster scrambled up onto the wing. He maneuvered across a scattering of glass and with a jump landed in a circular opening before disappearing inside. .

The sun was dipping low through the trees. Night would be here soon. Casseomae felt hungry after all the excitement of the thing falling in the Forest. She was eager to set off to forage. But then a scent hit her nose. A familiar scent. It had been nearly masked by the other strong odors coming off this strange relic. She sniffed, trying to identify it.

Blood.

"Hey, rat, I think—"

But before she got it out, there was a shrill squeal. The rat leaped out, knocking aside the broken glass as he landed on the wing. He tumbled to the edge and fell. Once he hit the ground, he ran, shooting through the underbrush and bracken.

Casseomae caught up with him in a thicket of cedars up on a bluff. The rat was trembling, his black eyes bulging more than ever. "What's the matter?" she asked.

"They . . . they're in there," he panted.

"Who is?" Casseomae growled. The rat blinked up at her but said nothing. "A wolf?" she asked.

"No," the rat whispered. "Old Devils."

"What?" the bear grunted. "What do you mean?"

Dumpster looked through the cedar branches at the silent relic lying crashed in the Forest. Then he said, "There are Old Devils in there."

CHAPTER FOUR

Casseomae had heard all sorts of stories about the Skinless Ones who ruled the Forest long ago. All the Forest clans, both vora and viand, had their own legends. They varied greatly, but all agreed the Skinless Ones had been ferocious monsters. Casseomae guessed the Faithful probably had different stories, but then their clans had served the Skinless Ones and had been under their protection.

"What do you mean, Old Devils?" Casseomae asked. "You saw bones?"

"Not bones," Dumpster said. "Bodies. They're all in these eggs made of glass. They've shattered, I guess from the crash, and those Devils, they're just lying around—"

"They're not moving?" Casseomae asked.

The rat was talking rapidly, almost faster than Casseomae could follow. "No. I was looking around at them thinking, Pluck my whiskers, I can't believe what I'm seeing! and, Hey, look, my da was wrong! They do have fur, but it's only a little tuft on top of their ugly heads, when all of a sudden I heard something clicking. I turned around, and there was this one glass egg that wasn't shattered. It was opening."

"Was a Skinless inside?" Casseomae asked.

"Do I look like a spittin' idiot? I didn't stick around to find out!"

A howl sounded from the Forest. It was answered by a chorus of other yips and barks.

"Those cur-licking coyotes again?" Dumpster asked.

Casseomae growled, "It must be."

The rat was staring at the strange relic. "Murk's whiskers!" he said. "Look!"

Casseomae nosed aside the cedar boughs to peer down. The last rays of sun cut low through the trees and illuminated the passering with an orange glow. The shattered window was mostly in shadow. But as Casseomae watched, a paw reached out, a pink furless paw.

Another paw felt around tentatively at the opening before a head emerged. The rat was right. There was a little patch of fur atop the head, a yellow-brown color almost like the winter grass in her meadow.

A coyote barked, louder now, closer.

"Am I raving, old bear?" the rat squeaked. "Look! A spittin' Devil, right there!"

"I don't think it's skinless," Casseomae said.

"Whiskers and snappers!" the rat cursed. "I told you that already. Who cares if it has feathers? Those Devils aren't supposed to be living! Don't you understand?"

The creature wiggled its way through the hatch and climbed down onto the wing. It was making whimpering sounds.

"What's that covering its body?" Casseomae asked. The creature seemed to have fish scales or some shiny lizardlike skin from its neck down.

"They're called clothes! But that doesn't change the fact that those . . . monsters are supposed to be all gone." The rat was circling in terror, its body racked with shivers.

"Dumpster . . . ," Casseomae began as she watched the creature walk unsteadily to the edge of the wing and look around at the Forest. "How big were the ones inside?"

"I don't know! Bigger than that one. How come?"

"It's just a cub."

"No! You think?" the rat squeaked.

"Yes."

Dumpster peered skeptically at the creature standing in the falling sunlight. The coyotes were coming closer, their whines and yaps growing louder.

"But what in the name of Lord Murk does it matter?" Dumpster said. "It's one of the Old Devils! It'll murder us all!"

"That little cub isn't going to kill anyone."

The creature stood listening to the barks of the coyotes with wide, fear-filled eyes. It looked around at the darkening Forest before backing up the crumpled wing.

The rat clicked his teeth. "Cub or not, it's one for the crows, as we always say. Those cur-lickin' coyotes will be here any moment. It's gone, old bear. I am too. I've got to find my mischief." Dumpster looked up at Casseomae, then turned and scurried away through the grass.

The coyotes broke through the underbrush and surrounded the wing. Casseomae watched as the little creature began calling out in some strange language, waving its small hands frantically. It might have been bigger than a coyote, but Casseomae had seen a rout of coyotes work together to take down an elk bigger than that little cub.

Something stirred deep in Casseomae's mind. An instinct coursed sharp and hot through her body—an instinct akin to the one that drove her to gorge in the fall or the one that urged her to nestle into her den when cubs had grown inside her. It was a pain within her tied to all those lost litters, all those cubs born breathless, all those cubs she had never been able to raise.

Casseomae bounded down the bluff, reaching the

coyotes in a few leaps. With a swipe of her paw, she caught Rend in the muzzle and sent the coyote tumbling end over end. Casseomae stood on her hind legs and roared. Half of the rout scattered back into the trees. The few that remained received such a volley of blows that they were soon scattered as well. The bear's jaws caught Rend by the hind leg as she tried to escape and flung the yelping coyote through the bushes and saplings.

Casseomae turned to the creature trembling on the wing. Something strange was happening to its face. Water streamed from its eyes across its cheeks. She gave the cub a little reassuring huff and put her front paws onto the wing. The metal crinkled beneath her weight.

As she leaned forward, the cub—this little creature who was no Devil, no monster, the little youngling who wasn't skinless at all—did not recoil. It watched her with wide, sky-colored eyes.

She bit it at the shoulder, picking it up in the gentle, firm way a mother bear picks up a cub. Her huge jaws could break a wolf's leg. But as she lifted the child, her teeth didn't even pinch it and the cub didn't cry.

She stepped down from the metal wing with the cub hanging from her jaws, limp and not making a sound. Casseomae lumbered up through the cedars and away from the crashed ship, setting off into the Forest with the first stars of the evening coming out.

CHAPTER FIVE

The Forest was alive with the night. Creeping steps. Flapping wings. Chirps and choruses, buzzes and breathing. In Casseomae's meadow, the child lay whimpering in the cinder-block den. Casseomae watched it from the crumbled doorway, wishing she knew how to settle the little creature into sleep.

Perhaps it needed to eat. With the moon rising over the treetops, Casseomae went out to forage. She buried her snout in the grass, searching for tender shoots, upturning rotten logs to get at the burrowing grubs. Gathering a mouthful of the grubs in her lips, she lumbered back to the den.

The child stopped crying and watched her with wide eyes. Casseomae made a huff and dropped the grubs before the child. It looked at the wiggling white larvae and then at her.

"You eat it," she said. "Doesn't your kind eat food?"

The child wrinkled its nose and pushed away one of the grubs that was worming closer.

"Maybe you don't like grubs." Casseomae sniffed at the child, trying to figure out if it could understand her. "Well, what do you eat anyhow?"

The child's breathing had settled. It stared at her, wiping its dripping nose with the back of its hand.

"Sure are leaky, aren't you?" she grumbled, backing out of the den. Once she stepped into the moonlight, the moaning resumed.

Casseomae hadn't been foraging for long before she realized the child's pitiful noises had stopped. She went back to the den. The child was sleeping. Casseomae gave a grateful snort and began to eat the grubs. "No," she said, stopping herself. "Might be hungry when it wakes." She lumbered out in the meadow, leaving the grubs wiggling in the dirt by the sleeping creature.

She watched her cave from the tall grass. What was she doing bringing this creature back to her den? She knew what these Skinless monsters had done to her kind and to the other clans of the Forest.

She wrestled with these thoughts until dawn broke. The sun was just rising above the trees when something rustled through the brush before her.

"You've not been eaten yet?" she said.

"I can take care of myself." The rat settled on his back legs before her. "What's your name again, old bear?"

"Casseomae."

He twitched his whiskers. "I'm Dumpster."

Casseomae grunted. "So where is the rest of your mischief anyway, Dumpster?"

"Think I'd be here if I knew?" He dipped his nose glumly. "I lost them. I was separated from the rest back in our city. Things were getting bad. Curs and lesser voras had been overrunning the place. Then our skyscraper fell. Busstop and Hydrant were killed right next to me. Who knows how many others? But Stormdrain and lots of the others escaped. I followed their scent out into the Forest—"

"Look, rat," Casseomae said, shifting her weight between her forepaws. "I don't understand half of what you're saying. What fell?"

"A skyscraper. It's an Old Devil building. Like this cinder-block den of yours, except bigger. A lot scratchin' bigger. They stretch up into the clouds."

Casseomae wondered if this could even be true, but then she'd never been to one of the Skinless's cities. "So where were they headed?"

Dumpster twitched his whiskers. "They'd talked about trying to find the Havenlands."

"Well, can't you find them there?"

"I could if there was such a place," he said with a sigh.

Casseomae grunted with confusion. "Why would your mischief go there if it isn't real?"

"Because without their Memory to advise them, they get idiotic. Stormdrain will never keep them thinking straight without me around. No, they're looking for the Havenlands for the same reason all those other feather-brained viand tribes are."

Dumpster blinked his beady eyes at Casseomae's confused expression. "Haven't you heard of the Havenlands? Of course you haven't. You're a vora. Well, rumors of the Havenlands have been circulating around the viands for a sun's age. Some say it's a mountainous city. Others say it's a meadow surrounded by impassable brambles. But all agree it's by the Wide Waters, and all agree the Havenlands is a place without voras. Herds and tribes of viands living unmolested. Plenty to eat and no danger can reach you."

Casseomae snorted. "A place where the wolves don't rule?"

"Yeah, I know," Dumpster said. "Sounds too good to be true. But Stormdrain is set on finding it. I've got to find them. Just like my da and his da before, I'm the Memory for the mischief. My rats need me."

"I don't understand," Casseomae said. "Memory of what!"

"Of the stinkin' Old Devils, you mushroom-brained bear." Dumpster snapped his tail irritably. "What've I been telling you? There isn't another clan of creatures, vora or viand, that knows more about the Old Devils than our kind. Our survival depended on it before the Turning and sure as spittin' depends on it now! Back in the last age, we lived among those Devils. We ate from their caches. We slept in the warmth of their dens. I'm not saying we were Faithful like some flea-ravaged cur or puss. We were thieves! And spittin' proud of it."

Dumpster rose as high as he could on his hind legs and wiggled his nose at Casseomae. "Since the Turning, we've gotten by on what was left behind. There's still Old Devil food to be eaten, if you know how to open a can. We do! We've figured out their water tunnels and valves, figured out how to open their boxes and doors, and figured out how to spill canisters of poisons to throw off pursuing voras."

Casseomae listened with interest but understood barely a word the rat was saying.

"Knowledge," Dumpster said. "That's our edge. You see? Like knowing Vorago. It's how we've survived. And to think of my mischief out there alone without me . . ." His words trailed off.

"So you know about these Skinless?" Casseomae grunted.

"Isn't that what I've been saying?" Dumpster squeaked.

"You know what they eat?" the bear asked.

"Been eating it my whole life," the rat replied with a cocky wiggle of his whiskers. "Or at least when I can get my paws on it."

"Come with me, then." Casseomae lumbered to her den.

Dumpster hesitated at the door. He lifted one paw and sniffed, letting his nose guide him up on his hind legs.

"What in the name of Lord Murk is in there?" Dumpster asked.

"The cub," Casseomae said.

"The . . . the Old Devil pup?" the rat piped. He was in a frenzy of agitation, circling back and forth, hopping and slapping his tail to the dirt. "You—you—no, you didn't! What's it doing here?"

"I brought it here."

Dumpster looked up at Casseomae, his bulging black eyes blinking in disbelief. "What did you do that for?"

"Rend's guard was going to kill it."

"So?"

Casseomae extended her lips irritably and gave a woof. "It's just a cub."

"It's a Skinless!" the rat shrieked. "An Old Devil. Do you have any idea what its kind did to us? Of course you don't. You mushroom-brained bears can't remember last moon."

"We have stories about the age before the Turning," she said.

"Then you should know what those Old Devil hunters did!"

"*That* cub didn't do anything," Casseomae growled. "You ought to have heard it moaning all night. Poor thing's hungry. Needs to drink too, I'd reckon. But all it's done is whimper like a blind newborn."

"What are you planning to do with it?" Dumpster asked.

Casseomae stood still. She hadn't thought exactly what she planned on doing with the creature. All she had known was that the coyotes would have killed it if she hadn't saved it. It was a cub, after all, not so different from the ones she had lost.

"It needs food," Casseomae said at last. "You know what its kind eats. Can you—"

A roar came from the far side of the glade. Casseomae turned and rose up on her hind legs to sniff. She dropped back down and said, "It's Alioth, my sloth's chief. You'd best—"

But the rat had already disappeared.

CHAPTER SIX

The bear chief blinked up at the bright sunlight, then stopped several lengths from where Casseomae sat in the doorway to her den. Alioth lowered his head, growing stiff-legged.

"You stink of it," he growled.

Casseomae watched him silently, showing respectful submission but not groveling or moving away.

"I suppose it's true, then," Alioth said. "The coyotes are telling of a living Skinless One that they captured and that you stole from them."

"They didn't capture the cub," Casseomae said.

"A *cub*, is it?" Alioth grunted. "How do you know it was a cub?"

"There's no mistaking it, Big One," Casseomae said, feeling she would know better than a battle-scarred male, even if he was wise like her chief. "The rest of its pack are dead. They fell from the sky in a relic just out there in the Forest. You can see it for yourself."

"I already did," Alioth said.

"Does the Ogeema know?" Casseomae asked.

"Rend was heading that way when I crossed paths with her." The bear chief stiffened angrily. "When she told me what you had done, I said that it was not possible. That my clan keeps nothing from me."

"Big One—" Casseomae began anxiously.

"My bears keep nothing from me!" Alioth roared. "We forage freely in the Ogeema's realm. Old Chief Megrez fought to secure that. We don't need to give the Ogeema a reason to revoke our pact."

"The Ogeema is a wicked fool," she grumbled.

"That may be, but do you want it like it used to be? Like it was for my mother?"

"No," Casseomae said softly. "I'm sorry. I should have come to you, Alioth."

The bear chief's stance slackened. He came closer and gave a forgiving snort. "Yes, you should have. You are dear to me, Casseomae, and I worry how you are treated by the rest of the clan. You cannot risk making yourself more of an outcast."

Alioth settled back on his haunches, sniffing once more at the air. "The creature's stink seems to have stuck to your glade. Did you kill it here?"

Casseomae hesitated. "I didn't kill it."

"What?" The chief lunged up onto all four paws. "You let it go?"

"No," Casseomae replied. "It is here. In my den. It sleeps."

A growl rumbled in Alioth's huge chest as he walked toward her. "Then move aside! So I can kill it and have this bothersome business over with."

Casseomae lunged at her chief. "You will do no such thing!" she roared.

Alioth quartered his stance, edging sideways from her. "You forget yourself."

"It is you who forgets, Alioth," Casseomae said. "Don't you remember? You were once like that little one in there. Alone. Helpless. In need."

"That is not the same—"

"Who protected you?" Casseomae continued. "Who got you through that winter? Who kept Megrez's jealous brothers from tearing you apart? I had just lost my first litter, and you were just an orphaned cub, thanks to the old Ogeema. I suckled you, Alioth, because you were just a tiny thing. And if I hadn't . . ."

Casseomae let her back muscles relax. Her bristled fur lowered. She eased a few steps out of the doorway. "If I had not taken the Skinless cub, Rend and her vermin would have killed it. I could not let that happen."

"No, they would not have killed it," the chief said.

"They would have brought the cub to Ogeema Dire as is demanded by law. You know as well as I that any of the Faithful must be brought before him. It is part of the pact."

"It's not a cur," Casseomae said.

"Exactly!" Alioth said. "This is much worse. Don't you realize the threat this creature poses to the Ogeema . . . to the entire Forest?"

"It's just a cub!"

"It's one of the Skinless. Those monsters drove the clans into the farthest reaches of the Forest. They killed us by the droves. If you think the Ogeema's rule is brutal, it is nothing compared to the cruelty of the Skinless Ones. We should be thankful to the Ogeema's ancestors for ridding the Forest of their kind."

"Those are nothing but lies," Casseomae said. "Legends spun by the wolves for their subjects. We don't know what the world was like before the Turning."

"Nevertheless, the Ogeema will learn of the cub before long."

"I'll fight whatever wolves the Ogeema sends," Casseomae growled.

"You are brave, old bear," Alioth said. "And strong. No doubt you could fight off many of their guard. But you remember why you had to take me in as a cub. My mother defied the old Ogeema. How many wolves did he send against her? Even if we stood beside you, our clan could not stand against the tide of wolves and voras that Dire commands. We would lose much more than our foraging privileges."

Casseomae looked back into the dark. The child was still sleeping. It was so helpless. And it was alone in the world . . . like she was.

"What should I do?" she whispered.

Alioth came close. He pressed the flat of his snout into her neck, nuzzling her fur. "Let me pass. It would be a mercy. Quicker than the Ogeema's wolves."

Casseomae shook her head. "I cannot." She paused, then said, "I will leave, and take the cub away from the Ogeema's realm."

The bear chief backed away, fear showing on his downturned snout. "This is madness," he said. "The Ogeema commands more than just the wolves and coyotes of this territory. His influence extends far beyond these borders."

"I know," Casseomae said. "But there is no other choice."

Alioth's dark eyes were sad. "Your heart has always been too strong. A mother's heart. You have until tomorrow. One way or another, the creature must be gone by then."

Casseomae watched Alioth lumber back across the meadow into the shadows of the trees.

CHAPTER SEVEN

Rend rarely ventured near the Ogeema's hall. Even at the Summer's End Offering, the coyote would hurriedly leave her rout's tribute of a fawn or some other viand and get as far away as she could before nightfall. As the towering hall came into sight, Rend's panting quickened and her heart thundered in her rib cage.

"Quit stalling, you whelps," she snarled at her rout.

Her mate, Gall, trotted at her side, but the rest of the rout—Pule, Plod, and Fest—were trailing farther and farther behind.

"We're nearly there," Rend said. "Once the Ogeema hears our news, we'll have nothing to fear ever again from his pack. We'll be heroes—"

Gall whined as the rout stopped sharply. Rend

surveyed the skeletons littering the Forest ahead. Picked clean and bleached by the seasons, the Gateway of Bones always made her feel as if she were seeing snow, as if winter never ended here at Dire's keep. So much white poking through the ferns. So many tributes brought before the Ogeemas over the ages. Bodies of viands going back until the Rising.

"Turn back if you're too cur-hearted to come with me," she growled. "But know that I won't share the Ogeema's reward."

Pule and Fest leaped away into the Forest. Plod hesitated for half a moment before joining them.

"Cowards," she yipped after them.

Gall flattened his ears. "Rend?" he said.

"What?" she barked.

"Behind you," her mate managed to say.

Several wolves paced toward them through the mist. When they had made a semicircle around them, the largest one growled. "What business have you here, yellow backs?"

Rend gathered her wits. Whimpering like a pup would only provoke the Ogeema's guard. She lowered her eyes respectfully and said, "We seek an audience with Ogeema Dire. We bring important news."

Another wolf laughed mockingly. "What would coyotes consider news? Is a blight of mange going through your rout? Is your fur falling out?"

Reflexively, Gall licked at his front leg where the rat had taken out a chunk of fur. In a wounded voice he said, "We've news meant only for the Ogeema's ears."

Rend stiffened at her mate's stupidity. She quickly said, "It would not do that the Ogeema's guard hears before he does."

The leader took a step forward. "Do you know how many mite-brained coyotes, foxes, and curs, as well as dirt-ranked wolves, come to waste Ogeema Dire's time with so-called news in the hope of winning favors? You tell us what news you have. If it is worthy of the Ogeema's attention, then we will deliver it to him."

Gall paced anxiously behind Rend. "We should go," he muttered.

Rend had to think quickly. The news of the Skinless One was too important to give away to low-ranking boneyard guards. She looked at Gall. "Yes, you're probably right, my nipper. It would not do getting the Ogeema angry with these fine masters."

The leader growled. "Angry? Why would the Ogeema be angry with us?"

Rend let her tongue drop slackly from her jaws like some half-wit cur. "Let us waste no more of your time, cousins. Especially on nonsense from the bears."

"Bears?" the wolf asked. "Where do you range, coyotes?"

"In Chief Alioth's domain," Rend said. "We try not

to give credence to anything a bear has to say, but it is hard not to listen when he slights the Ogeema."

"Insults Ogeema Dire!" one of the other wolves growled. "Who is insulting our father?"

Rend dipped her eyes shamefully. "If we share news of something Chief Alioth said, wouldn't you be duty-bound to report it to the Ogeema?"

"Of course," the leader said.

"And—forgive me, for I have never met nose to nose the esteemed ruler Dire—isn't his temper legendary?"

The wolves glanced at each other uncertainly.

Rend turned to Gall. "Let us go, my dearest. Best that we keep Alioth's words to ourselves."

The pair had trotted no more than a few steps before the leader of the guards barked sharply. "Come with us, you two! You are to report to the Ogeema immediately what you have heard."

As they were led toward the Ogeema's hall, Rend heard one of the guards chuckle to another, "It's been a long time since I've seen the Ogeema bite the nose off a coyote. I can't wait to see this."

Gall whimpered and licked a swift pink tongue over his wet snout.

As they crossed over a rise, they left the Gateway of Bones and entered the Field of the Fallen. Perfectly preserved skeletons of ancient wolves covered the field, wolves who had fought in the Rising. And among them were the remains of their defeated foes—the Skinless Ones.

Some of the skeletons were lying in open-topped wooden boxes. Others lay on the ground. These bodies had been set out on display by the Ogeema's ancestors so that all would remember what the legendary Ogeema Taka-Dirge had done during the Rising. How he had gathered all the packs of the Forest into an army that had slaughtered the last of the Skinless right here on these sacred grounds. Ever since, the Ogeemas had used the neighboring building as their den.

The Ogeema's enormous territory and his influence over the other packs and clans of the Forest were founded on this story. But if the end result of the Rising was somehow in dispute, then what would happen to the Ogeema's rule?

Anxiety rose in Rend's belly. She would have to be careful how she revealed this news. To suggest that the legend was wrong—that Taka-Dirge had not killed the last of the Skinless—might incur Dire's wrath. Maybe she should have let the guards deliver the news after all.

Rend looked at the guards surrounding her and ahead at the towering den. Wolves—more wolves than she had ever seen together in one place—lay around the exterior of the stone structure. Some wrestled with one another. Some slept. A few watched her impassively as she and Gall passed them.

There was no turning back now. To gather her courage she reminded herself that the reward could be immeasurable if she played it right. But if she incurred the Ogeema's wrath, she would have to hope her and Gall's deaths would be swift. She knew they would not be so lucky.

"Look up," Gall whispered to her.

The exterior of the den was covered in ivy and vines. A few exposed portions showed that the structure was built in the Skinless's fashion of stacked stones. From the roof of the den rose an immense spire, taller even than the surrounding trees. At the top Rend spied a solitary wolf poking his head through the tangle of ivy.

"How do they get up there?" Gall gasped.

Before she could reply, the wolf high in the tower howled. His call was instantly answered by the wolves surrounding the den. Even the guards leading them stopped to add to the tremendous sound. Gall sank to the ground, terror paralyzing him. Rend listened as barks and howls echoed from the surrounding woods. Wolves innumerable cried out the Ogeema's name, warning any who heard their chorus that they would die upon a thousand teeth if they entered their domain.

Rend had heard this call before, but only carried faintly on the wind. As terrifying as it was, she knew it was purely ceremonial. None who heard the call would consider taking up against the Ogeema's army.

As the last of the chorus died away, the guards led Rend and Gall into the den. Rend was surprised not only by the enormity of the space but also by its dimness. She had been in caves—many where she had birthed litters—but they were tight and comfortable. Never this cavernous! She had also been inside the Skinless's ruins, but they were mostly open to the sky. The Ogeema's hall was the most perfectly intact Skinless structure she had ever entered.

Along both sides of the long space were faintly glowing panels of every imaginable color. Some were broken, and through them Rend could see the wall of ivy that covered the outside of the den. The hall was deeply shadowed, and nowhere more so than the far end where they were being led.

The guards stopped just before they reached an area where the floor was higher. Atop the rise, immense wolves—much bigger than the guards and any of the wolves outside—lounged about, a few lifting their ears or heads as the guards approached. A scattering of rolling pups snapped at one another in playful bundles.

Behind the wolves lay an alcove of utter darkness. Rend could hear breathing coming from the darkness, and while she could not see the wolf inside, she knew it was the Ogeema.

The guards backed away, all except their leader. "My general," he said.

The wolves on the rise turned to the dark alcove. The pups ceased their games. Rend heard a strained sound slip from Gall's throat, and she feared her mate might make a suicidal dash for escape. She gave him a quick nip on the top of his nose.

A voice spoke from the dark. "What season is it, guard?"

"My Ogeema?" the guard asked.

The Ogeema's voice was not the guttural snaps typical of a wolf. The words were whispered, but the power in that barely present voice unnerved Rend to her core.

"The season. I asked what season it is in the Forest."

The guard hesitated a moment before saying, "Near High Summer, my Ogeema."

A pair of eyes appeared in the shadows. One was golden and the other was a pale sky-silver. Rend thought for a moment the Ogeema might be blind in the pale eye, for she had heard the Ogeema was deeply battle-scarred from his rise to power in the pack. But as she looked closer she saw the dark pupil in the center and realized his eyes were simply two different colors.

"It isn't yet Summer's End?" the Ogeema breathed.

"No, my Ogeema." The guard looked with confusion to the other wolves atop the rise, but they said nothing.

The eyes moved closer. For a moment Rend thought the eyes were simply hovering in the darkness. Then, as a set of white teeth flashed briefly, she understood that, unlike the rest of the gray-coated wolves, Ogeema Dire's fur was black.

He stepped out from the alcove, moving so silently and gracefully that he could have been mist. Circling around Rend and Gall, the Ogeema paused before the guard, who was only half his size. "Well, this is most generous of you . . . what is your name, guard?"

"Goad," the wolf replied.

"Yes, forgive me, Goad. Of course. This is kind of you to bring your Summer's End tribute early." The Ogeema eyed Rend and Gall hungrily. "You clearly know my weakness for yellow backs. I will enjoy them immensely."

Gall's back legs gave out, and he whimpered as he tried to rise again.

"My Ogeema," the guard said. "No. I'm sorry, I didn't bring them for you to . . . what I mean, my general, is these coyotes bring news. From Chief Alioth's range."

The black wolf's eyes narrowed. "The bears?"

"Yes, my Ogeema."

The Ogeema glared at him. "You could not have carried their message to me, guard?"

"Well, yes . . . but I thought it best for you to hear it directly from them, my general."

The guard cringed, but the Ogeema said, "Very well. Return to your post." The Ogeema watched Goad as he and the other guards trotted away. The Ogeema's mismatched eyes lingered on them until they were gone. Without turning his head, the Ogeema asked, "Have the pickings grown so scarce in Chief Alioth's range?"

Rend didn't realize the Ogeema was addressing her until he turned to look at her.

"What do you mean?" she asked, remembering to add, "My Ogeema."

"You want something. Usually it is better hunting grounds. The few that have managed to outwit my guards to gain an audience with me often ask to be allowed the last of the carcasses after my wolves are finished. Food. That's what it often comes down to, doesn't it?

"If it's not better eating you seek," he continued, "maybe it is territory. The others in your pack are attacking your young, or maybe it's my wolves?"

"I'm not here for that, my Ogeema," Rend said.

"But you're here for something," the Ogeema whispered. Rend noticed a pale scar beneath the fur at Dire's throat and wondered if it was the cause of his quiet voice. "They always come to me wanting something. But it is customary to offer some token. What have you brought me, coyote? Is it your companion?"

Gall collapsed.

"No, my Ogeema," Rend quickly said. "This is my mate. I apologize that I have no token to offer you, but you will understand once you hear what I have to say."

The Ogeema growled, circling Gall, who had rolled onto his back with his legs limply sticking up as if he were already dead. "I care nothing for gossip, coyote! Whatever you have overheard Chief Alioth blabbering is worthless to me."

"It is not gossip I bring," Rend said, considering whether she would defend Gall if the Ogeema sank his teeth into his exposed stomach. He was a terrible coward, but he was the father of her pups, after all. To win the Ogeema's favor, however, might be worth his life.

"My guard said—" the Ogeema began.

"I lied to him," Rend interrupted. "What I have to tell is too important to give to any lesser wolf, my Ogeema."

The Ogeema turned from Gall. His expression changed. His jaws relaxed and his ears perked up. "You have gravel guts, don't you, coyote?"

Rend felt pleasure at this but knew better than to let a compliment get the better of her. She had to stay focused and to use all her cleverness and courage. "I admit I have no love of the bears," she said. "And if what I tell you drives them from my territory, then I won't whine."

"So speak, coyote. And quickly, while your presence still amuses me."

"My rout knows well, my Ogeema, how the great Taka-Dirge led his army against the last of the Skinless

45

Ones. The Forest—voras and viands alike—are grateful to your ancestors for the Rising."

"Yes," the Ogeema said.

"My mate and I saw something disturbing just a day ago."

"What did you see?"

"You know of the relics that the Skinless Ones flew? The great silver birds that lie rusting in the Forest?" She paused, not expecting the Ogeema to answer but wanting to make sure he was following her words. "One fell from the sky."

The wolves behind the Ogeema flicked their ears curiously.

"We were there when it landed. And from inside appeared a Skinless One. A living Skinless One."

In an instant the wolves atop the rise were on their feet growling and glaring ferociously at Rend. The Ogeema stood motionless.

Rend continued. "I know as well as any that they were all slaughtered. But a Skinless has been sent down from the sky. To the bears."

"To the bears?" the Ogeema whispered.

"We set upon the Skinless One, my Ogeema," Rend said. "My rout and I. We were going to bring the creature to you, but a bear stopped us. She is called Casseomae. She fostered Alioth as a cub when his mother was killed."

"Yes, I remember."

"Casseomae protected the Skinless from us. She's taken the young Skinless to her sloth."

"Has she now?" the Ogeema said. He stepped onto the rise, pausing to lick one of the pups between the ears. When he looked back at Rend the Ogeema's expression was calm. "You might have guts of gravel, coyote, but your tongue drips with viper poison."

Rend flattened her ears.

"There are no Skinless Ones being sent down to the bears. It is simply not possible."

"But, my Ogeema—" Rend began.

"Whatever grievance you have with Chief Alioth is not my concern. And bringing me lies won't tempt me to involve my wolves in your dispute."

"I'm not lying!" Rend yipped.

The Ogeema snapped his enormous head around.

"My Ogeema," Rend said. "Please, I will bring you proof! A piece of the fallen relic."

"Some trash you'll dig up, most likely," the Ogeema breathed as he slipped back toward the shadows of his alcove.

"My Ogeema, if you would simply—" Rend started to say.

But the Ogeema cut her off. "Get away while you still have your breath and be glad I've lost my appetite.

Bring me the Skinless One if you want to offer proof. Otherwise, I don't want to smell you or any of your rout again. Do you understand?"

Gall was on his feet, nipping at Rend's muzzle to leave. She stared a moment longer at the black wolf before saying, "Yes, my Ogeema."

She trotted off after her mate, slinking low with disappointment.

Once the pair was out of the den, the Ogeema said to one of his wolves, "If she's speaking the truth . . ."

"Should I send a patrol to investigate, my Ogeema?" the wolf asked.

"No," said the Ogeema. "I don't want Alioth pestering me with complaints about violating the pact. We must send someone Alioth will never notice in his territory."

The Ogeema lowered his snout to his paws, looking up with his gold and silver eyes.

The wolf thought a moment, then said, "The assassin?"

The Ogeema bared his teeth. "Yes, the assassin." He closed his eyes. "Send him."

CHAPTER EIGHT

Casseomae watched her chief until he disappeared back into the Forest on the other side of her meadow. When she turned, she found the cub staring at her from the doorway of the den. She came toward it and the cub whimpered in its strange chirping speech.

"It's safe, cub," Casseomae said. She rubbed her nose against its cheek, trying to settle its panic. She stuck her nose in the den. "You didn't eat your grubs. You've got to eat. You've got to have strength if we're going to get you away from here tonight."

Casseomae spent a few minutes digging up dandelions from the glade and gathering mouthfuls of acorns. She even managed to catch a vole, but as she brought each to the child, it pushed them away with chirps of protest.

Casseomae sighed and was about to try something else when she caught the child putting its mouth to its upper arm. At first, she thought it might be licking a wound or cleaning the strange furless pelt covering its body. But then she heard a slurping noise.

She edged closer to see what the cub was doing. A tube protruded from its hide. There were lots of the strange protuberances and pouches along its body, none of which made any sense to her. As she watched, the cub's cheeks drew in and its throat lumped with a swallow.

It's drinking, she realized. But how could the creature drink moisture from its own body? She shuffled away a short distance to sit down and think.

This was no bear cub—this was a Skinless One. It was unlike any creature in the Forest. She couldn't communicate with it. She couldn't understand it. What was she doing protecting it?

The cub took its mouth from the tube and settled back against the doorway of the den. It looked up at the sky, where the clouds were turning orange and pink with the setting sun.

It needs me, she reminded herself.

She heard something coming through the brush beyond the nearest of the vine-tangled cars. Something scraping along the ground. "Haven't you been eaten yet?" she called.

"Nice to smell you too, you big lump," Dumpster called from the thick grass. "How about coming over here and helping me?"

"What's the matter?" she said, lumbering toward him.

"Nothing's the matter. I've only been dragging this stinkin' thing halfway across the Forest."

As Casseomae pushed aside the weeds, she spied the rat pulling something with his teeth—a square container with the distinctive sheen of the Skinless objects.

"What is that?" she asked.

"It's plastic. A material the Old Devils could make."

"I've seen it before. Why are you carrying it?"

"It's for the cub," Dumpster said before going around to the other side and pushing against the box with his head to scoot it forward.

"For the cub?" Casseomae asked.

Dumpster twitched his whiskers. "Yeah, for the cub. The Old Devil over there." He sighed. "To eat."

"They eat plastic?"

"No, you idiot bear. The food is inside." Dumpster gnawed at a corner with his teeth before prying at the top of the box with his narrow paws and popping the box open. Inside were neatly stacked rows of small shiny packages. Dumpster pulled one out and dropped it before Casseomae.

She lowered her nose and sniffed. Dumpster had

perforated the package with his teeth, and a strange, sweet odor came from inside. "There's hardly enough in here for a meal."

"It's plenty, believe me," Dumpster said. "A little goes a long way with this Old Devil food."

"Where did you get these?"

"From a squirrel's nest," Dumpster said in his acid tone. He snapped his tail and pointed with his nose. "I got it from that crashed passering out there. The cub won't eat our food. I've seen the remains of their food caches back in my city and believe me, the Old Devils hardly ate anything that we scratchin' eat. They like this stuff. Go ahead. Give it to the pup."

Casseomae picked the crinkling package up with her lips. The plastic left a bitter taste in her mouth, and she was glad when she was finally able to drop it before the child. The child sat up sharply, its eyes fixed on the package.

Dumpster scampered to peer from around the bear's back leg. "What's it doing? Did it eat it?"

"Not yet. It's not even touching it. Are you sure that's food? It tastes awful."

"Yeah, that's just the wrapping. They used plastic shells to protect their food. Trying to keep us rats from eating their cache." Dumpster looked up, giving a smug twitch of his whiskers. "We got into it anyway, of course. Idiot Old Devils."

"Look," Casseomae said.

The child reached for the food. In an instant, it tore off the crinkling casing and bit greedily from the sweet-smelling lump.

"You were right," Casseomae said.

"Course I was right. I told you I'm the Memory for my mischief. I know all about these Devils."

The rat watched her for a moment before saying, "What are you doing anyway, old bear? I mean, that's a stinkin' Old Devil sleeping in your den and you think you're going to make a bear of it?"

"It's not an *it*," she said, suddenly realizing it herself. "It's a *he*."

Dumpster gave her a skeptical twitch of his whiskers.

"I can just tell," she said. The cub had a sort of stubborn, rootlike smell. A smell like a thundercloud on the West Wind. A smell not unlike Alioth's when he was a cub.

"We'll be leaving soon," Casseomae added.

Dumpster blinked rapidly. "You're taking him away?"

"That's right."

"To where?"

"I don't know yet," she said. "Somewhere the Ogeema won't find him. But the first thing is to get him out of my sloth's range."

Dumpster glared at her. "You are one moon-mad old

bear, you know that? When Lord Murk was giving out brains, he stuffed your head full of moss."

Casseomae huffed. "What are you going to do? Will you look for your mischief?"

The rat's whiskers drooped glumly. "When I left the city, I had their scent. But then those underlickin' coyotes made me lose their trail."

"You'll find them," she said. "If they're anything like you, they're surely stout rodents."

Dumpster gave a little shrug of pride. "I guess."

Casseomae sniffed toward the child. "What about traveling with us?"

Dumpster gave a scoffing squeak. "Right."

"I could use you," Casseomae said. "You know all about the Skinless. And if you're with me, you won't have to worry about every owl and skunk coming after you."

Dumpster wiggled his whiskers as he considered her words. "I don't much care for the idea of being around some murderous Skinless," he finally said. "But that little pup over there seems harmless enough. I guess I could come with you. For a little ways. At least until I pick up the trail of my mischief."

The cub swallowed the last bite. Tracing a finger along the inside of the package, he drew out the last morsels and licked them off his fingertip with noisy smacks.

"Then the first thing we have to do," Casseomae said, "is figure out how to get that cub to come with us."

Dumpster scampered around in a circle cheerfully. "I think I know just the trick. Watch." Dumpster pulled out another package of food. "Give that to the pup."

Casseomae picked it up and eased over to the child with a reassuring snort. He looked at the packet in her teeth. When Casseomae dropped it, the child ran forward and grabbed the food.

"Now just wait," Dumpster said. "Once the pup finishes, he'll want the rest. Don't let him have any."

"But he's hungry," she said.

"Of course he is! That's the point. Pick up the box when he comes for it. You got it?"

"What do I do then?" Casseomae asked.

"Start walking."

"Where?" she grunted.

"Scratchin' mites!" Dumpster squeaked. "Don't you understand? The pup will want the food. If you carry it away, he'll follow you. Then we can lead him out of here."

The child stuffed the last bite in his mouth and looked around. When his eyes fell on the case of food, he ran toward it.

"Now!" Dumpster squealed.

Casseomae lifted the case in her mouth. The child

grabbed at the bottom of the box, but Casseomae jerked it away and growled.

"There you go," Dumpster said. "Now walk."

Casseomae took a few steps. The child stood with his arms limp at his sides. She snorted, "Come on, then, cub."

"He doesn't understand Vorago," Dumpster said.

"I know he doesn't," she grunted through her clenched jaws. As the child began to come toward her, she added, "But it seems he understands food."

Dumpster trotted beside her. "I told you he would."

CHAPTER NINE

As long shadows fell, Casseomae and Dumpster led the child away from the meadow with the setting sun at their backs, toward the borders of the Ogeema's territory. At first, the child chirped incessantly at her and even tried to tug the case from her mouth. When frustration drove the child to sit on the ground, Casseomae gave him another packet. After eating, the child followed them again. Little by little, they made their way deeper into the Forest.

Casseomae was surprised by how much difficulty the child had simply walking. Vines snagged his arms and legs. Logs and fallen branches seemed intent on stumbling him. She'd never seen a creature move more awkwardly through underbrush. It was as if the Forest was trying to prevent the child's journey . . . and Casseomae half-wondered if the Forest really was.

The child had an unreasonable fear of everyday noises. When a chorus of cicadas rose up, the child looked around in panic. If a tree frog croaked or a blue jay called, the child leaped in fright. A squirrel caused him to shriek as if he had fallen into a nest of timber rattlers.

After a few hours of chirping piteously for food and battling every spiderweb and leaf that tickled his head, the child calmed somewhat. They covered little ground that first day.

It was late in the night before Casseomae decided to stop. "I can't carry this wretched-tasting thing one more step."

"The pup is asleep on his feet anyway," Dumpster said. "We'd better let him rest."

Casseomae placed the container next to the child, offering him another meal, but the cub was already curling up in the leaves. Within moments, he was asleep.

"You'll keep your nose up?" Dumpster said wearily.

"Yes," she said. "I'll know if anything comes near. You get some sleep."

Dumpster dug out a little den in the leaf mold. Casseomae foraged for a bit before joining them in sleep. When she woke in the morning, the child was already awake, adjusting the pouches around his waist. He watched Casseomae from the corners of his eyes.

She stood and stretched, calling, "Rat, you ready to go?"

Dumpster emerged from the damp leaves, blinking at the bright light.

Casseomae loped over to the container of food and bit down. It came up much too easily. She dropped it.

"What's the matter?" Dumpster asked, digging out beetles from a rotten log.

"It's lighter," Casseomae grunted.

The rat dashed to the box and slipped his head inside. "It's scratchin' empty!"

They looked at the child.

"Does that pup look fatter?" Dumpster asked.

"He couldn't have eaten them all already," Casseomae said.

"He didn't. He's got them hoarded away in his pouches."

Casseomae bumped her nose against the child's side. She felt stiff lumps and heard plastic crinkling. The child swatted at her and dashed several strides away, making funny noises in her direction.

"What do we do now?" Casseomae asked.

"That bare-nosed sneak can go lick himself for all I care." Dumpster snapped his tail in aggravation. "Either he comes with us or he doesn't. I'm just ready to keep going."

"How do you figure we'll get him to follow?"

"Why do I have to come up with all the spittin' ideas?" the rat complained.

Casseomae lumbered toward the child. "Come on, now."

"He doesn't speak Vorago, acorn brain," Dumpster called.

Casseomae nudged the child with her nose, urging him to walk. But the child ran in circles, turning her attempts into a game of chase.

Dumpster watched in near disbelief. "You look like a pair of half-wit curs."

As the child swooped past her, Casseomae caught him by the tuft of material between his shoulder blades. The child flailed, crying out angrily, but Casseomae held tight.

She strode past the wide-eyed Dumpster and snarled through her clenched teeth, "You coming?"

After a while, the cub relented and walked, although not nearly at the pace Casseomae would have preferred. They foraged as they followed the rising sun. While they saw none of the larger voras, they were never far from viands who weren't happy to see a Skinless One in their Forest. Squirrels called down angrily from branches overhead. Families of deer watched in confusion as the child passed. Birds fled.

After a few more times being carried, the child settled into a silent march, staring down at his feet and following the bear. If the cub stopped for more than a moment, a woof from Casseomae had him walking again.

By midday, they reached a creek with steep banks. Casseomae drank beside Dumpster, while the child squatted on a boulder, fidgeting with something between his shoulder blades.

"What's he doing?" Casseomae asked.

Dumpster watched as the child removed a clear bag from his back. A tube connected back to his arm.

Casseomae grunted in horror. "He's pulled his own entrails from his body!"

With a pop, the child disconnected the tube and dipped the bag into the stream. Bubbles rose to the surface.

"It's not entrails, old bear," Dumpster replied. "It's a device."

"A what?"

"A device. Like the box for its food. The Old Devils don't drink from streams or puddles like us. Watch."

After a moment the child reattached the tube and slid the bag into the fold on his back. The child put his lips around the tube protruding from his shoulder and took a deep drink.

Dumpster gave a squeaking laugh. "See! It's for drinking."

The child undid a flap on his leg. Casseomae half-expected blood to spill, for raw muscle to be exposed, but the interior was the same shimmering blue as the outside. The child took out a package of food, pulled it open, and began eating the lump from the crinkling covering.

Casseomae felt her muscles relax. The cub was strange, but not so appalling once she understood his ways.

She followed Dumpster across the creek, but as they looked back, the child remained squatted on the rock.

Casseomae grunted irritably. "We've moved at a toad's pace all morning."

"Well, then pick the pup up again!" Dumpster said.

"And contend with his racket?" She was tired of it. A mother shouldn't have to tote her cub. A cub should obey. But she supposed he wasn't really her cub.

The child ate the last bite of the food and dropped the package to the ground.

"Let's just start walking," Dumpster said. "He'll follow us."

"I don't know," Casseomae said, feeling a knot of unease in her breast.

"Trust me, he won't want to get left behind."

Dumpster began climbing up the mossy embankment. With a backward glance at the cub, Casseomae ascended after him. About halfway up, she said, "He's not coming. I'll have to carry him."

Dumpster stopped and rose on his hind legs, sniffing.

"You'll have to be a lot taller than that if you want to scare the cub into walking," Casseomae muttered.

"Your nose is better than mine, bear. Don't you smell that?"

Before Casseomae could catch the scent, she knew instantly she should have trusted her instinct not to leave the cub. A pale gold form slipped silently from the bracken behind the child. The creature slunk forward with the kind of grace and precision that only cats have.

But this was no mere puss. This was a cougar, and one of the biggest ones Casseomae had ever seen.

CHAPTER TEN

Casseomae barreled down the embankment. The child sprang up in fright at her sudden approach, slipping on the slimy boulder and toppling into the creek. Casseomae hit the water with a splash and rose up on her hind legs as the cougar struck, his teeth catching the edge of the child's blue hide, barely missing his neck.

Casseomae smashed her massive paw against the cougar's head. The cat tumbled into the creek, howling and throwing up a spray of water. Sitting up, the child saw the cougar for the first time and screamed. Casseomae moved between him and the cougar and roared, angry spirals of saliva dripping from her teeth.

The cat leaped to the side, but Casseomae bit down on his thick tail and slung him away. The cougar yowled as he came at her again, this time twisting in midair and landing on her back. He sank his teeth into her neck.

Casseomae had fought cougars before. When it came to a carcass, she could drive the big cats away without blood being spilled. Cougars were quick to determine if they had the advantage and were not ones to take injuries over a simple meal.

This cougar was not after something to eat. He fought too ferociously. And in that instant, she remembered Alioth's warning and understood. This was the Ogeema's assassin.

Although she felt blood spilling down her neck, Casseomae wasn't worried. Her throat was thickly armored with fat. She could withstand this assault a little longer.

The cat clawed at her face, searching for her eyes. Roaring, Casseomae stood on her hind legs and fell back, hoping to break the cougar's ribs. But the cougar let go before he landed and leaped away.

Casseomae jumped to her feet. The child was running away, already out of the creek and climbing the embankment. He was fumbling for something in one of his pouches. The cat was right behind him.

With blood in her eyes, Casseomae charged after them, knowing she would never reach the cub in time.

As the cougar lifted a paw to strike, the child turned

and held up a small object. It flashed a bright blue light in the cat's eyes.

The cougar reared back in alarm. Casseomae fell on him, biting to the bone in the cougar's back leg before pinning him to the ground with her paws on his back.

"Did the Ogeema send you?" she roared.

Dazed, the cougar rolled his eyes in pain and spat, "What are you doing, wicked bear? Don't you see what danger it brings? You would forsake the Forest for this Skinless devil?"

Casseomae flinched at the cougar's words. In that moment, the cougar slipped out from beneath her. He scrambled to the top of the embankment and disappeared into the Forest, his back leg dragging.

Casseomae sniffed the child for injuries, but he was unharmed. He sat on the embankment with the little glowing object still in his hands and stared at Casseomae. His sky-colored eyes filled with moisture and sent streams down his face. He chirped something to her quietly.

"You're safe, cub," she breathed. "He's gone." She licked his salty face to calm him. The cub didn't flinch from her, but he did wipe his arm across the place where she'd licked.

"Cass," Dumpster said as he scampered up from the creek bank. "You're still in one piece. That cat was a nasty one! I haven't seen another like him. Are you hurt? You're bleeding pretty badly."

Casseomae turned her neck side to side and licked her long tongue across her snout. The wounds would heal. Pain barely registered for her.

"The cub is alive. That's all that matters."

"No, all that matters is that we get out of here," Dumpster squeaked, "before he comes back!"

"He won't come back," Casseomae said. "The Ogeema sent him. The cougar missed his chance."

Dumpster looked wide-eyed at the child before scrambling after him and Casseomae. It wasn't until the three were winding their way through the massive trunks away from the creek that Casseomae realized the child was walking by her side. A feeling of satisfaction crept into her. He was acting like a good cub now.

By nightfall, they reached a tree marked with deep scratches down the bark.

"What do those mean?" Dumpster asked.

Casseomae gave a huff of relief. "We've reached the border of Chief Alioth's range. And if we're leaving my sloth's range that means we're also leaving the Ogeema's territory."

"But whose territory are we entering?" Dumpster asked.

Casseomae licked again at the crusted blood on her snout before lumbering forward. "I don't know," she said.

CHAPTER ELEVEN

That night they slept in the ruins of a burned-out building. Dumpster disappeared under a sheet of rusted metal, while the child lay down against a brick wall not far from Casseomae. Later, with the moonlight coming down in silver streams through the trees, Casseomae rose to forage for moths. As soon as she stood, the child sat up and whimpered.

"I won't go far, cub," she said. "Keep sleeping."

When she ambled away, the child followed her. "Go on back now," she snorted. But the child would not leave her. She caught some of the fluttering brown morsels before returning to the ruins so the cub would get some rest.

After he lay back down, the child took something from one of his pouches. It was the object he had used to startle the cougar. A square of light appeared, casting a bluish glow onto the cub's face. Casseomae snorted curiously. The cub said something to her and then fidgeted with the object.

It looked like a piece of the sky, blue and steady and peaceful. Maybe the cub had brought a part of his home with him, she thought. Something to protect him from danger.

Her eyes grew heavy with sleep. When she looked up a little later, the square of light was gone, and the cub was sleeping.

Later in the night she was woken by a scent. The moon had set, and the Forest was dark and resounding with insect song. She stepped from the ruins. The acrid smell was from a canine. It could have been a wolf or a coyote or even a fox. She wasn't certain. What was important was that it wasn't the cougar. And it couldn't have been one of the Ogeema's wolves, not yet. The assassin wouldn't have had time to get back to the Ogeema and report what had happened.

But when the Ogeema found out, what would he do?

The cougar would surely report that they were traveling away from Chief Alioth's range. Hopefully the sloth wouldn't be punished for her crime. And hopefully when the Ogeema learned that the Skinless One was nothing more than a cub, he would lose interest.

But Casseomae realized that she herself was troubled

by the cub. The cougar had said the cub brought danger to the Forest. Could he? Cubs were helpless, but cubs grew into powerful warriors, just as Alioth had. What if this cub grew up to be a monster, like the Skinless Ones from the stories?

She gave an angry snort. No matter what he became when he was grown, there would only ever be just him. One Skinless couldn't harm the Forest. And she would raise him to honor and love their home.

The idea surprised her. Saving the cub from Rend and Alioth was one thing, but raising the cub as her own was another. She had seen many winters. She had lost all her own cubs. This might be her last chance. If she could only bring him somewhere safe. But where?

As she turned to go back inside, Dumpster emerged. "How do you expect a rat to sleep with all your stomping around?" He sat back on his haunches. "What's troubling you, Cass?"

Casseomae snorted. "We've left the Ogeema's territory, but we'll be in another pack's territory before long. They might even pay tribute to the Ogeema. If the Ogeema sends word to look for the cub, how can I ever hope to get the cub somewhere safe? Unless . . ."

Dumpster twitched his whiskers. "Unless what?"

Casseomae peered down at him. "Those Havenlands."

The rat's black eyes bulged. "Have you been eating toads?"

"You said yourself that your mischief is looking for them."

Dumpster flattened his whiskers. "Well, my da always said, '*When you're out of choices, better to run for the shadows than to wait for a hole to appear.*'"

Casseomae sat in silence a moment. "You said that the Havenlands are rumored to be by the Wide Waters. Which way is that?"

"The same way we're going," the rat said. "The same way I followed my mischief out from the city. Toward Sun's Birth."

"Then that's where we'll go," Casseomae said.

Dumpster twitched his whiskers, but he didn't argue.

CHAPTER TWELVE

The following afternoon they were passing through an area with a surprising number of relics when Dumpster gave an excited squeak and hurried ahead.

"What do you smell?" Casseomae called, but the rat had already disappeared through the underbrush.

As she and the child followed, Casseomae found that the vegetation gave way to smooth slabs of stone she'd seen before. Dig down in her meadow, and there was this sort of Skinless's rock. It made the ancient paths that crisscrossed the Forest, trails that were now half-buried under dirt and leaves and vegetation.

When she reached Dumpster, she saw they were standing on one of those paths, but one much bigger than any she'd seen before. Toward the setting sun, side-by-side trails of broken rock disappeared into the

Forest, each path as wide as a river. Surveying the other direction, Casseomae was amazed to see that the twin paths rose above the treetops.

The rat scampered around the decaying relics, sniffing furiously as he climbed up the slope. Casseomae hesitated, having never been above the trees. When she caught up with the rat, he was at a place where the Skinless's path had collapsed. The path resumed a short distance away across a gap. The child lay on his belly to peer down over the broken edge at the debris and giant slabs lying in the Forest below.

"What is this thing?" Casseomae said.

"This, my mossy-brained bear, is a highway," Dumpster said.

Casseomae snorted. "The name fits. It certainly is high."

The child cried out, his voice echoing across the landscape.

Dumpster said, "This is the way to go. Stormdrain would want to follow a highway. A little piece of the city out here in the Forest, you see."

"Well, we can't go over the edge," Casseomae said.

"Course not, mushroom brain. Get the pup." He scampered back the way they'd come.

At the bottom of the hill, they turned and traveled beside it until they'd passed the hole in the highway above. After a time, the path descended until it rejoined the Forest floor. In places it was consumed by vegetation and earth.

All along the way there were rusted and vine-strangled relics. The child touched their frames curiously as he passed them. "What did the Skinless Ones use these relics for?" Casseomae asked.

Dumpster twitched his whiskers importantly. "For moving around. Sort of like that passering starship the cub came down in, except these cars only went on the ground. That's why they made highways."

Casseomae considered this. "Why? Couldn't they walk?"

The rat gave an amused squeak. "Well, of course they could walk. Look at that pup there. He walks. But he's only got two feet. How do you expect him to move fast on two feet?"

"I've seen him run pretty fast," Casseomae said.

"Cars helped them go even faster," Dumpster said.

"Why were they in such a hurry?" Casseomae asked.

Dumpster scampered ahead. "Scratch if I know, old bear."

They followed the highway as long shadows stretched down their path. Once the sun had set, Dumpster skittered to Casseomae's side. "Hey, Cass, I smell something."

"I smell it too," she said. "Something follows us, but don't—"

Dumpster spun around. The damage done, Casseomae looked back as well. She saw a shadow shift as a creature disappeared behind a rusted-out relic far down the highway.

"You see it?" Dumpster asked.

"Yeah," Casseomae grunted as she started walking again. "I saw it."

"Is it the cougar?"

"No, it's not the cougar."

Dumpster skittered in erratic leaps and scampers. "So what is it? Coyote?"

"Too big," Casseomae said. "Probably a wolf."

The child walked along, glancing curiously at a large sheet of metal that hung above the highway. Casseomae looked back over her shoulder, but the highway behind them was empty.

"Could be a scout," she grunted. "We must have entered a pack's territory."

Casseomae slept uneasily that night. Every bird woke her. She paced around the sleeping child, catching the occasional waft of the canine scent. The creature had not moved on around them in the night as she had hoped but lurked out there in the darkness.

She settled near the child, who was splayed in the leaves in the most vulnerable of sleeping positions, on his back with his belly exposed. With her snout, she nudged him onto his side. He didn't wake, but as he curled up next to her he reached out to settle a hand on her forepaw. Casseomae licked at his fingers to soothe herself as much as the murmuring cub.

Strange. They were more similar than she would have thought. His fingers were in many ways like her claws. Not so powerful or deadly, but he could do agile things with those narrow fingers, just as she could pry open a mussel shell or tear off bark. And she and the cub both stood on their hind legs and could walk that way too. Wasn't it odd that bears could do that when wolves and deer could not?

The Skinless Ones were ancient enemies of the Forest, but this little cub was so weak. He had none of the natural weapons given to the creatures of the Forest, no fangs or claws or antlers. He hadn't even been able to smell the cougar and only realized it was there when it was already on him. She supposed it was their devices that had allowed the Skinless Ones to dominate the Forest. But the cub's little device did nothing more than flash a surprising display of light. That would do little to protect him from the voras who would want him dead.

Casseomae's concern for the cub made her restless. It made her want to keep moving, to flee, which was a strange and unfamiliar sensation for a bear. But the impulse to get the cub away from harm, to keep him safe, was some deep-down tug she couldn't contain.

In the morning, Casseomae and Dumpster foraged as they traveled, and the child—never close enough to touch Casseomae but never more than a quick dash away—ate one of his lumps of food.

Casseomae found herself having to listen to Dumpster's endless lectures on the artifacts and relics they passed: poles strung with wires that carried electricity to feed the Skinless Ones' devices, billboards that had established territories along the highway like scent markings, gas stations for their vehicles to drink foul-smelling chemicals, and on and on.

She understood only the vaguest notions of what the rat was talking about, but she endured it all silently and kept a close eye on the cub as she smelled the creature following them.

By midday, they reached a creek, where the highway rose up again. Once, the highway had spanned the creek in what Dumpster called a bridge, but the bridge had long ago collapsed. As the child filled up his drinking device and Casseomae lapped at the cool water, the rat said, "We're still being followed, aren't we?"

A rumble of aggravation sounded from Casseomae's throat. "What I want to do is hide the cub and go fight this scout once and for all. Get it off our tails."

"The pup would never do that. He might keep his distance, but he's been stuck to you like a briar since that cougar."

"I know," she growled. "And if I went back after this wolf, it would simply run away."

"Only to bring back its pack," Dumpster added. "But why hasn't it done that already?"

"I don't know. Maybe it's a low ranker who wants to capture the cub and get rewarded. Either way, there's only one reason I could guess why it hasn't attacked yet. It waits for an advantage, a moment when I'll leave the cub alone."

Dumpster twitched his whiskers. "Then I scratchin' suppose you'd better go ahead and do just that."

Casseomae nodded. "Tonight, after the cub is asleep, I'll move away from him . . . not too far, but enough to lure that wolf closer. You'll have to help me keep watch."

"Ugh, I'm barely getting any sleep as it is," Dumpster complained. "Out here with all this . . . Forest. I miss my cozy sewer pipe back in the city."

"Your what? No, never mind. My head can't hold another new word."

That evening they reached a place where the highway split and one part rose to curve around the other. Because the overpass had collapsed, it formed a sort of concrete cave underneath. With only one way in, Casseomae felt she would have no trouble smelling when the wolf arrived and defending the cub.

"Keep your nose high," she reminded Dumpster as the child lay down to sleep.

The rat scrambled under a bit of rocky debris. Casseomae waited until the cub's breathing grew heavy and then crawled up to the uppermost recess of the cave. It was cramped, but the narrow space, along with the peculiar odor of the cub, would mask her scent from anything outside. Once the wolf entered, she could easily descend upon it.

She waited with painful anticipation. Several times her eyelids grew heavy, but at the first sound of sniffing, she was awake, all her senses honed. The creature tramped on the highway overhead. For a moment Casseomae thought it had missed them entirely, but then the snuffling returned, and she heard the creature coming down through the brush.

Casseomae waited, letting the creature get closer. As it slunk through the entranceway, she realized something didn't smell right. This wasn't a wolf. But what sort of canine was it?

A sharp screech erupted, and a shadow flashed up from the ground at the intruder. The vora yelped and spun in circles. Whatever it was, Dumpster had locked on to its muzzle.

The child woke with a shout. Casseomae bounded down to block the cave entrance as the cub slid behind her. The creature shook its head until Dumpster came loose, flying over to land at Casseomae's paws.

Casseomae peered through the shadows at the

cornered vora pacing back and forth. "What is it?" she asked the rat. "Can you tell?"

"Yeah, I can spittin' tell. Got its Faithful stink all over my tongue." Dumpster slashed his tail angrily. "Vilest of vile. Can't you see, Cass? You've trapped a cur!"

CHAPTER THIRTEEN

The creature made to dash around her, but Casseomae swiped a paw. "Stop!"

Having come into the glow of the moonlight, the cur was visible now. Its coppery-red fur was shaggy and bramble-knotted. One ear was missing entirely. Flattening itself, the cur panted, "Pray, bear, let me pass. I mean you no harm."

"Why are you following us, dog?" Casseomae demanded.

"I haven't been following you."

"Liar!" Dumpster squeaked. "We've smelled your stench for two days now."

The dog bared his teeth at the child hiding behind Casseomae. "What is that? What is that creature?"

"Don't even look at him," Casseomae warned.

"It's true!" The dog rose and stepped forward. "It's one of the—"

Casseomae roared, raking her claws across the hard earth, sending the dog back.

"He's here to take the pup," Dumpster said. "Probably wants to offer him to the Ogeema as a tribute."

"Why would I do that?" the dog barked.

"Tired of being despised by every vora in the Forest," Dumpster said. "Desperate to win favor and make amends for the sins of your scratchin' kind. Old bear, you know what you have to do."

"Shut your squeaking, little mouse!" the dog snapped. "You don't know what you're talking about."

"Mouse? Did you just call me a mouse?" Dumpster's tail lashed furiously. "Oh, that's it! I'm ripping off that other ear—"

Casseomae dropped a paw in front of Dumpster. "Stay where you are."

"You don't get it, Cass," Dumpster cried. "That cur's a Faithful. He's just found his new master. He won't stop until he can steal the pup away for his pack."

"I have no pack," the dog said bitterly.

Dumpster clicked his teeth. "Liar."

"They were killed," the dog said. "By the Ogeema's guard. Only I survived. I have nothing left. Just let me go."

"Don't look for pity from us, cur." Bristling his whiskers at Casseomae, Dumpster whispered, "He may not seem it, but that cur's dangerous. My da always said, *'Desperation makes killers of katydids.'* There's no telling what he'll do or when he'll be back for the pup. Best finish him and rid ourselves of the worry."

The dog dashed, but Casseomae cut him off again. The dog lowered his head, looking up at her with piteous eyes. "Please, let me pass. I mean no harm to any of you."

Casseomae heard the desperation in the dog's whine. He had to fight simply to stay alive, because his kind were hunted and despised by all the inhabitants of the Forest. This dog was an outcast. Casseomae knew what it meant to be an outcast.

She backed onto her haunches, opening a passage. "Go."

Dumpster squeaked, "No, you idiot bear!"

She put her paw down on his tail, holding Dumpster in place as she addressed the dog. "But if I see you again, dog, I'll figure you're here to hurt the cub—"

"I'd never hurt a Companion!" the dog barked.

Casseomae glared at him. "Go before I let the rat loose on you."

With a quick glance at the child huddling behind Casseomae, the dog scampered out from the cave with his tail tucked and disappeared into the night. The child ran to the entranceway. He called out and then turned back to Casseomae, chirping rapidly.

"Probably mad we drove off his slave," Dumpster mumbled.

"Come back in here, cub," Casseomae said. She nudged him gently with her snout. The child stared out into the dark for a few moments before lying down.

Casseomae plopped to the ground, blocking the entrance.

As Dumpster shuffled under the debris, he said, "I've got a bad feeling that cur will be back."

CHAPTER FOURTEEN

They traveled along the highway through the morning with no scent or sign to suggest that the dog was following them, but Casseomae could not get him from her thoughts.

A Companion. That's what the dog had called the cub. Before the rat and the cub, she'd never known what it was to have companions. Except for the spring feasting, the fall matings, and her time spent rearing Alioth many summers ago, she had lived a solitary life.

Bears did not enjoy the tribal companionship that viands like deer and rabbits shared. But the dog was not so different from the wolves or coyotes, who stuck together in packs. With his pack killed, did the dog think he could form a new one with the cub?

"Why are the curs considered the Faithful?" she asked Dumpster.

The child was ahead of them, swinging a thin metal stick he had broken from a car and hopping around like a frog from one side of the highway to the other.

Dumpster trotted beside Casseomae. "Because they served the Old Devils."

"I know that," she grunted. "But I've heard that hogs, for instance, were servants to the Skinless Ones back in those days. They're not hated like curs or even called Faithful."

"It's different," Dumpster said. "Those clans were captives. They were slaughtered for meat. But curs lived *with* their Skinless masters. They ate their food. They helped the Skinless hunt the rest of us down."

Watching the child playing ahead, she said, "Any signs of your mischief?"

"Not yet," he panted.

"You sure this is the right way?"

"Sure I'm sure. They might be traveling out in the Forest beside the highway. Stormdrain would know better than to risk being in the open. Too easy for voras to sniff his mischief out. They're out there. We'll find them."

Casseomae heard the hesitation in his voice but decided not to say anything.

At midday, she foraged chickweed, while the child ate

more of his food, tossing the wrappings to the ground. Dumpster was nosing through the leaves for seeds when he scared up a bright green anole.

Dumpster chased the lizard around the underbrush until it disappeared through a crack in the side of a car half-buried under a fallen tree. As the rat barreled through the narrow gap to follow it, the side of the car moved in a squeal of rust and shut. A moment later, Casseomae heard the muffled cries of the rat, and she lumbered over to investigate.

Through an unbroken square of glass, she could see Dumpster batting his nose against the surface, his eyes wide with panic.

"What's the matter?" Casseomae snorted. "Where's the lizard?"

"Scratch if I know," he squeaked. "I'm trapped! The door . . . it closed."

"The what?"

Dumpster gave her a venomous look. "The door. That . . . Just get me out already."

Casseomae sniffed at the car, searching for a way to get to the rat, but somehow the relic had sealed Dumpster inside. She pressed her paws against the glass and pushed. The clear surface bowed a little under her weight but didn't break. "I can't open it," she said.

Dumpster scampered back and forth inside. "There should be a latch. A metal part that you can turn."

"A latch?" she said.

"Yes, a latch, you idiot! I don't have time to explain about these Old Devil devices. Just look. Right down there somewhere," he said, jabbing his nose to the bottom edge of the glass. "Don't you see it?"

Casseomae sniffed along the frame. There was a part sticking out, not nearly as rusted as the rest, but she didn't know what to do with it. She bit at it, like she was prying the shell from a turtle, but nothing happened.

She backed up in frustration as Dumpster lashed his tail angrily at her. "I don't know what you want me to do," she said.

"I want you to get me out of here!"

The child came up beside Casseomae, putting his hand on her back. He chirped something at her as he grabbed the part with his delicate fingers and gave it a turn. She heard a click, and then the child tugged open the door with a screech of rust. Dumpster dashed out as the child held it open. He wiggled his whiskers at the cub and then ran from the car.

"Don't you want the lizard?" Casseomae called.

"It ain't worth it," Dumpster said, licking his front paws and shivering.

Casseomae looked over at the grinning child and gave a snort. The child plucked another package of food from his side, broke off a piece, and tossed it down to Dumpster.

Dumpster eyed the lump and then nibbled gingerly at it. "Not lizard, but it's not bad," he murmured before finishing it off.

The air was still and muggy as the three began a hard climb up the highway.

"That vermin-ridden Faithful is following us, you know," Dumpster said, scampering up beside Casseomae.

"I know," Casseomae grunted. "I smell him."

"The cub likes him," the rat said. "That's not good."

Casseomae grunted.

"You are trying to figure out a way to get rid of that cur, aren't you?" Dumpster said.

Casseomae grunted again. She wasn't sure what to make of the cur. He was a Faithful, and that meant he was a traitor to the Forest. But she was protecting the cub, so what did that make her? She knew she couldn't have the dog continuing to follow them. It would only bring trouble. But she felt a certain pity, admiration even, for this tough and lonely creature.

As they reached the top of the climb, the cub wiped his brow. The tuft of hair atop his head was wet and dripping down his face. Casseomae didn't remember the child dipping his head in a stream, and it certainly hadn't rained. "Why is he so wet?" Casseomae asked.

"Got me." Dumpster rose on his hind legs and sniffed. "We've got to run that cur off—" He began waving his long nose back and forth more vigorously.

"What is it?" Casseomae asked.

Dumpster scampered a few steps, sniffed, and then ran rapidly toward an overturned car. "Look! Look!" he cried.

Casseomae came over. "What?"

The rat was sniffing at a scattering of black pellets hidden among the weeds. "They're droppings. From my mischief!"

"Are you sure?"

"I know!" the rat said, his black eyes bulging wide. "I know my own mischief. They came through here. Not so long ago. Come on."

Dumpster ran ahead down the highway, dashing from bush to relic and keeping close to cover as he went. Casseomae and the cub followed him toward a collapsed bridge over a creek, where Dumpster stopped with a shrill curse. There was fur everywhere and black spots speckling the grass.

Casseomae sniffed. "Blood."

"They were attacked here," Dumpster said, his teeth chattering with fright. "I smell weasel all over this place."

Casseomae lifted her nose. "It's not here anymore."

The rat followed a faint scent trail into the underbrush off the highway. He had just disappeared in a thorny cane of blackberries when he gave a cry. Casseomae trudged around the bramble with the child at her side until they were on the bank of the creek.

Dumpster backed out of the blackberry cane dragging a rat with his teeth.

"Is he alive?" She snorted. But the rat was stiff and crusted in blood.

Dumpster let go of the rat's scruff and bumped noses with him once. "Tarmac was our best scout. One of Stormdrain's sons. Probably fought off the weasel while the rest of the mischief escaped. Oh, poor Tarmac. You're in Lord Murk's den now, brave buck."

The child knelt over the dead rat and touched a finger to his tail.

"At least the others got away," Casseomae said.

Dumpster sniffed. "Yeah."

"And we're on the right path, so—" she began before hearing panting and running paws coming from the highway. She rose quickly on her hind legs as Dumpster disappeared into the brambles and the child got behind her. "It's him again," Casseomae snorted.

The dog yipped as he went into the cane and then rustled his way around.

Dumpster poked his head out, clicking his teeth angrily. "What's it going to take to get rid of that Faithful piece of mite-infested cur?"

As the dog appeared, Casseomae growled, "I thought I told you—"

"A patrol of coyotes," the dog barked rapidly. "Just over the hill."

CHAPTER FIFTEEN

"A re they coming up the highway?" Dumpster asked, springing out from the brambles.

The dog cocked his head. "Highway?"

"The trail! The spittin' trail back there."

"No," the dog said.

The child seemed oblivious to their urgency and squatted to pet the dog's head, clearly happy to see him again. The dog licked the child's hand, giving Casseomae a cautious look. He then pointed his nose with a front leg cocked. "They're out in the trees. Over that way."

"Did they smell you?" Casseomae asked.

"I don't think so. I'm not sure. They were distant still and I had the high ground."

"Let's move," Dumpster said, his shock over finding

his dead mischief mate giving way to action. "We've got to get away from the highway. Follow the creek bed. It's an old mischief trick. *'Stay in the puddles and the voras it muddles,'* as my old da always said. They'll have a harder time picking up a scent in water."

Casseomae snorted. She wasn't feeling as concerned as the rat and dog seemed. These were only coyotes, after all, not the Ogeema's wolves or his cougar.

The dog began splashing downstream and the child followed him. Casseomae lumbered after them in the creek with the rat leaping behind her from rock to rock. When they got farther from the highway, Casseomae rose on her hind legs.

"Anything?" Dumpster panted.

"Hard to say," she replied.

The creek twisted and turned until at last it ran through a section thick with laurel. A covey of quail took flight from the trees ahead and flew toward them.

The dog stopped in the creek. "The coyotes scared up those birds," he whispered.

"They're up ahead," Dumpster said. "I don't know if they've smelled us or not, but they're up there."

Casseomae wasn't sure how to proceed. She wasn't used to hiding from other voras. This was not part of her instinct.

The dog held his nose high, sniffing, while the child kept one hand on the dog's back, looking around wide-eyed and seemingly more aware that something was amiss.

"How many were they?" Casseomae asked.

"Five, I think," the dog replied.

"I'll fight them," Casseomae said. "Five coyotes are nothing to me."

"You old fool bear," Dumpster said. "Quit thinking with your claws! It's got to be Rend's rout. If those coyotes see it's you, they'll know sure as scratchin' that the pup is near."

"I can drive them off," Casseomae growled.

"They'll split up," Dumpster said. "And most likely send back word of what they've found. You might bust noses on a few coyotes, but you can't take a whole patrol of wolves!"

She knew this was true. While her every muscle craved a fight, she realized the rat's approach was more sensible. "So what do we do?" she asked.

"We just need to hide somewhere they can't smell us," the dog said. "Follow me."

He trotted into the thickest part of the laurel grove.

A yip sounded from over a rise: the unmistakable call of a hunting coyote. The child looked up at the sound and then over at the dog crouched down in the laurels. When the dog gave a pleading whine, the child got down on his knees and crawled to him.

The dog called, "Get on in here, old bear. Not likely

they'll smell you down here in this creek, but if they come over the hill, you'll be spotted."

Casseomae eased into the thicket beside the cub. "And what now?"

As Dumpster scampered in, he cast a look of loathing at the dog but then settled down into the leaf bed. "What else is there to do? We wait."

Casseomae dropped her chin to her forepaws, snorting irritably. She hated this. It felt strange. She watched the child rub the dog's coppery fur, and the dog stared at him bewildered.

"It's . . . remarkable," he said. "I've journeyed far across the Forest. I know every tree and relic. But I've never heard tell of a living Companion or even one who remembers the days when they ruled. The Companions are gone! And yet here before me . . . please, I have to know. Where did the pup come from?"

"Not a scratchin' word, Cass," Dumpster murmured.

But Casseomae did not share the rat's distrust of the dog. He had warned them of the coyotes. He could be useful. And the cub clearly liked him. However, there were more important things at the moment than satisfying the dog's curiosity.

She lifted her head. "You've traveled far in the Forest, dog? Where can I bring the cub where he will be safe—?"

A bark rang out from the top of the rise, answered by a yip.

"They're getting closer," Dumpster whispered.

Casseomae shifted anxiously, digging her claws in the earth. "Cursed Rend and her rout! If she reaches us here, I'll tear them apart."

"They'll never fight you," the dog said. "It won't do any good."

More calls echoed through the Forest, growing nearer to the top of the rise.

"Well, there's no other choice," Dumpster spat. "They're coming. She's got to drive them off."

"There's another choice." As the dog stood, the child sat up on his knees. The dog looked at Casseomae. "You'll have to keep him from following me."

"Where are you going?" she asked.

"I'll draw that rout away," he said. "They don't know I'm with you."

"You're not with us!" Dumpster said.

"Hold on to the pup," the dog said, ignoring Dumpster. "You understand?"

The child was watching the dog anxiously, a hand on his back. Dumpster clicked his teeth. "Stupid Faithful and his charms over the pup. He'll make an awful racket when you go."

"I'm not casting any spells on the pup," the dog said. "You ready?"

Casseomae huffed, inching closer to the cub. "Dog, tell me. Isn't there somewhere safe from the wolves?"

"If there were," the dog said, "why would I be here?"

He eased out from the thicket. The child leaned forward to follow, but the dog growled at him. A coyote called out just over the top of the rise. The child blinked rapidly at the sound.

The dog was out from the laurel thicket. He lifted a leg to spray urine on the outside branches. He trotted around and did it again. "Don't let him follow me, you understand?"

"We know!" Dumpster said, twittering his whiskers anxiously. "Get going."

"Bear?" the dog said.

"What?" Casseomae growled.

"If I were you, I'd ask the Auspectres your question."

"The who?" she asked.

A coyote bark rang out. The dog gave one last look back at the child and then in a blur sprinted up the rise toward the call.

The child leaped forward, snapping laurel branches. Casseomae lunged for his back and caught the blue hide with her teeth, not puncturing the material but not letting him go any farther either. The child called out and tried to scramble forward, but Casseomae had him.

Through the trees came booming barks, not the cries of a coyote but what Casseomae knew had to be the dog. His barks echoed through the Forest and soon were joined by the yowling, yipping coyotes converging on him.

The child shouted several more times and batted Casseomae's nose. She didn't growl but held him until the sounds of pursuit disappeared into the distance. The child reached back to tug the blue skin from Casseomae's teeth, and she released him. The child emerged from the laurels and stared at the Forest.

"We'll never see that cur again," Dumpster said as he scampered beside Casseomae. "But I'll have to give it to him. He's brave. Stupid, but brave."

CHAPTER SIXTEEN

The child continued to look around for the dog as
they followed the creek. Casseomae smelled no
sign that Rend's rout was following them, but she knew
they had to cover ground fast. Dumpster gave a squeak,
struggling to catch up. "You've got to move faster, rat."

"Look, I'm not a blundering locomotive like you,"
he said.

"A what?" Casseomae grunted.

"Nothing." Dumpster sighed. "I'm going as fast as I
can."

Casseomae cast an anxious glance. "If they catch
our scent . . . Look, just let me carry you." She reached
down with her long lips to pick Dumpster up by the
back.

He scrambled away from her. "Like some suckling

pup? No, no, no. Dumpster will not be slobbered on by a putrid-breath bear."

"Well, I'll leave you, then," she growled.

"Argh!" He lashed his tail. "Let me just climb on your back."

"What?" She snorted in disbelief.

"Look, you've got plenty of fat for me to hang on to. I'll just ride on you." Dumpster flattened his whiskers at her stares. "I don't like the idea any better than you do, old bear, but there's no other way for us to go faster."

Casseomae flopped down on the ground. "Just until we know we're not being tracked."

Dumpster climbed up her front leg, digging his tiny claws into her fur until he reached the massive hump of muscle at her shoulder. She rose and sniffed back at him. "Comfortable?"

"Not in the least," he said, digging his claws in a little tighter. The cub gave Dumpster a baffled look. "What are you looking at?" Dumpster squeaked.

Once she was moving at a faster pace with the cub jogging beside her, Casseomae asked, "Have you heard of those Auspectres?"

Dumpster jostled on her back. "No, never," he grumbled. He crept closer to her ears, finding a better hold away from her bucking shoulders. "It's probably some Faithful rumor. Just get us back to the highway,

Cass. We know my mischief went that way. We need to follow them."

As night fell, Casseomae sat atop some boulders listening while the cub filled his water pouch at a spring. Night birds and tree frogs filled the darkening Forest with their chorus, but there was no sign of the dog.

Dumpster trotted out on the boulder beside her. "We have a problem," he said.

"What?"

"I think the pup is out of food."

Casseomae gazed down at the child. He was licking a shiny wrapper, but she saw that the pouches along his belly and legs were no longer bulging. "What do we do?" she asked.

Dumpster flicked his whiskers. "Nip me if I know. I guess we hope we find an undiscovered Old Devil cache."

"Is that likely?" Casseomae asked.

"No," Dumpster said.

She snorted and lumbered down toward the child. "We should go. Too easy to be sniffed out on this high ground. A little farther and we'll rest for the night."

The following day, Casseomae watched the cub closely but never saw him take out more food. By midmorning, the tuft of golden fur on the child's head had turned wet again. The heat drove Casseomae to scratch against the rough bark of trees, much to Dumpster's displeasure.

"I'm riding up here," he complained, crawling on her head to avoid being squashed.

A startled rabbit dashed from a log right in front of Casseomae and she brought her huge paw down on it in a flash. As she stopped to eat the surprise catch, Dumpster leaped from his perch to search for a meal of his own. The child flopped to the ground, squeezing water from the tube onto his face.

By the time Casseomae had eaten the rabbit, she found that the cub had stripped the blue hide from his torso and arms. She watched with a mix of horror and fascination. Without his hide, the cub was pale, bare, and deer-thin. He was hitting the blue hide with a sharp rock.

"Don't do that to yourself, little cub," she warned, nudging his bare back.

The cub shot up when her wet nose touched him and chirped in his funny speech before going back to work.

Over and over the cub prodded the hide with the rock until the fabric tore apart. Dumpster emerged with an acorn in his mouth just as the child was putting the clothes back on. The parts that had been covering his arms were now gone.

Casseomae sniffed at the two limp pieces lying on the ground. They looked like shed snake skin. "Is this why they're called the Skinless? Because they can remove their hides?"

"It's not his hide, mushroom brain," Dumpster replied. "I told you before. It's clothing. The Old Devils didn't grow it on their bodies. They made it to keep warm."

"Does your memory tell you why he just tore part of it off?"

"Probably for the same reason you've been rubbing against every tree in the Forest."

"I'm getting off my winter coat," Casseomae said, feeling an itch arise at the mention.

"There you go," Dumpster said smugly. "Our pup here is just trying to cool off."

"Humph," Casseomae snorted, feeling much better about the whole situation. "They were pretty clever creatures, weren't they?"

"Yes, they were," Dumpster said, crunching on the acorn. "Too clever, if you ask me."

The child watched as Casseomae bent down to nose up an acorn and eat it. He came over and put an acorn tentatively in his mouth. When his teeth crunched on it, he immediately spit the broken shell out in distaste.

Casseomae watched with concern. "He's so bony as it is. We've got to find something he can eat."

"His kind ain't fit for Forest food," Dumpster said. "They ate beefs, cousins of the deer but bigger and slower and stupider. Unfortunately the wolves wiped them out long ago."

"I could catch him a fawn," Casseomae said. "Maybe he'd eat that."

"Old Devils never ate fresh kills. They stuffed the meat in containers called cans. Tough to open, but of course we figured out how!" Dumpster twitched his whiskers smugly. "Old Devils loved eating birds, too, but they had to be set on fire and I've got no memory for how to do that."

Casseomae considered the cub's predicament as they continued. Was it hopeless to expect that the child could live off the offerings of the Forest? Was his kind really so different from the tribes of voras? Could they only survive with canned foods and false hides and devices and relics?

By nightfall, purple thunderheads had risen behind them and rumbles pealed through the trees. After the heat of the day, Casseomae didn't mind the prospect of a wet night. The rain began with white flashes of lightning, sending the child closer to her. A sharp crack of thunder erupted, shaking the ground.

"It's safe, cub," Casseomae snorted gently to the whimpering child, and then added to Dumpster, "I'd figure if he came from the sky, he'd have seen storms worse than this—"

"The highway!". Dumpster leaped from her back and sprinted ahead over rising puddles until he stood on the path's hard, cracked surface. "At last, we've found it again."

As Casseomae lumbered up onto the highway, she paused to sniff. She peered through the gray falling light and rain. "That's not all that's back."

The child gave a shout and began running toward a coppery-red form lying under the shelter of an overturned vehicle. When Casseomae caught up, she feared the dog might be dead. He was lying on his side with blood in his fur. But when the child knelt next to him, he opened his eyes. "You found me," he gasped.

"Not on purpose," Dumpster said.

"The Companion has been led back to me," the dog said, clearly pleased as the child nuzzled his fur and chirped softly to him.

"Murk's whiskers," Dumpster mumbled.

"Are you badly hurt?" Casseomae asked. "How did you escape Rend's rout?"

"Rend," the dog scoffed, licking the child's hand before continuing. "Is that her name? A more vicious coyote I've never met. Fortunately she keeps poor company. Her mate and guards have no more sense than doves and hardly any more courage. I escaped with only a few bites but none so deep."

"Then why don't you get up?" Dumpster said. "If a vora had come across you before us, you'd be in a poop pile of trouble, wouldn't you?"

"He's plainly exhausted." Casseomae flopped to the still-warm highway as the rain soaked into her fur.

Standing out in the pouring rain, Dumpster turned his black eyes from the dog to Casseomae. "Then let's go before he can follow us. If we set off now—"

"You'll be washed away in no time," Casseomae grunted. "We'll rest here for the night."

"With this cur?" Dumpster said in disbelief.

"He helped us."

"That Faithful vermin didn't help me. He helped the pup."

The dog lifted his head. "You call me a Faithful, rat, and yet you're the one traveling with a Skinless One. You're helping him as well."

"I'm not helping him," Dumpster squeaked.

"You found him that Skinless food," Casseomae reminded him.

"That's not the same!" Dumpster clicked his teeth angrily. "Besides, even if I was helping this here pup, that doesn't make me a Faithful. Feeding a lost pup isn't the same as serving in the army of the Old Devils. It isn't the same as helping those murderers wage war against the Forest tribes."

The cub stared with owl-wide eyes as Dumpster

skulked off toward another car not far away, then he crawled in next to the dog, out of the rain.

Casseomae expelled a sharp snort of air. "Ignore him, dog. He has a foul temper since he lost his mischief. Probably had it before then too."

"His words don't hurt me. I've kept my oath and soon I'll be rewarded."

"Oath?" Casseomae grunted.

The dog struggled up onto his forepaws. "Tell me, bear. Where did this pup come from?"

"You won't believe me."

"I scarcely believe the pup is real, even with his paws upon me."

"He fell from the sky," Casseomae replied.

The dog cocked his head. "You mock me. Like the rat, you think since I'm a Faithful—"

"I've got nothing against you, dog. And I'm not lying. Even the rat saw it. They fell—"

"They? There are other Companions?"

"They're dead," Casseomae said.

"Was it the Ogeema?" the dog asked, a slight growl in his breast. "Did he kill them?"

"No. They died from the fall. Only this cub survived."

"But there could be others, couldn't there?" the dog barked. The child looked around sleepily before lowering his head back to his arm. As his eyes closed, he reached out to pat the dog's head. "The pup could lead us to them," the dog said.

"The cub is lost," Casseomae said. "He doesn't know where to go. I've barely been able to get the pitiful thing to follow me."

The dog continued to lick happily at the child's hand. The cub pulled it away with a few chirps of pleasant complaint before rolling over to fall back asleep.

The dog grinned widely at Casseomae. "My clan tells of a day when the Companions will return. When we'll be reunited and our persecution by the Ogeema and his kind will be over. But only if we remain faithful and keep our oath of loyalty until they return. And now they've returned! Now they are coming back to us, coming back home."

"There are no other Companions," Casseomae said. "I told you he's the only one."

"You're wrong," the dog replied. "There are others. There have to be. And the pup will lead me to them."

CHAPTER SEVENTEEN

As morning light spilled across the highway, the rain evaporated from the leaves in a steamy mist. The dog was up and scampering around. The child chased after him, calling out his own strange and happy barking noises. Dumpster emerged to join Casseomae where she had dug up an ant mound.

"I assume you're not running him off for a reason."

"I can't protect the cub alone," Casseomae said. "I need the dog."

"You need that dog like you need a flea in your ear," Dumpster said. "I'll be scratchin' glad when I find my mischief. Then I can leave you to watch that pair of tongue-lappers run around in circles."

Casseomae peered at the child and the dog playing

together. Their grinning expressions did make them seem akin.

The child leaped on top of a relic. His clothing-hide was opened at the chest, and the bottoms were rolled up to his knees. With the arm portions now cut away, he looked like he was molting—shiny blue giving way to a slightly fuzzy pink-white. But all of it was taking on the brownish hue of dirt. The cub had grown filthy since his arrival and last night's rain only made it worse. The Skinless certainly didn't know how to stay clean like the Forest's cubs.

The dog trotted over and said, "We'd better not follow this trail. Too many voras and viands use it."

"Well, this is the way we're going," Dumpster said. "If you're too cur-hearted to follow us, you can go another way."

The dog bristled but tried to pointedly ignore the rat. "Why are you following the highway?" he asked Casseomae.

"His mischief is going that way," Casseomae said. "In search of a safer territory. I'm hoping it will lead me to a safe territory too. For the cub."

"Until the Companions take back their place, there is no safe territory in the Forest for his kind," the dog said.

"What about the Havenlands?" Casseomae asked.

The dog flattened his ear and glanced over at

Dumpster. "You've been listening too much to that rat. The Havenlands don't exist."

"First of all," Dumpster squeaked, "I told that mushroom brain that the Havenlands don't exist. So don't accuse me. Second of all, eat droppings!"

"I have to find somewhere," Casseomae said. "What was it you said before about the Auspectres?"

The dog looked with sidelong wariness at the cub resting against a poplar trunk. "I'm not sure it was a good idea."

"Why not?" Casseomae asked.

"It's . . . too dangerous."

"More dangerous than wandering the Forest?" Casseomae growled.

When the dog hesitated, Dumpster said, "I told you it was cur nonsense."

"The Auspectres are witches," the dog said quickly. "Carrion hunters. By eating the dead, they can divine what is to come."

"I don't like this," Dumpster said.

"Well, the cub isn't yours!" the dog snapped.

Dumpster lashed his tail. "He's not yours either, no matter how bad you long for a Companion."

"Right," the dog said, his hackles twitching. "He's the bear's, and his fate belongs to her. I'm not suggesting we go to the Auspectres. Believe me, if I never have to see them again, I'll be grateful."

"So you've been to them before?" Casseomae asked.

"Once."

"Why?" she asked.

"Same as everyone who braves those witches," the dog replied. "I had a question."

"What did you ask them?"

He glared sideways at Dumpster. "I don't want to say."

"But what they told you," Casseomae asked, "were they right?"

The dog shrank a little, his remaining ear flattened. "Yes. They were right."

Casseomae felt a surge of strength fill her body. She rocked back and forth eagerly. "Then let's go. Let's see them now."

"They don't live near here," the dog said.

"But you know how to find them?"

"I do."

Casseomae nudged the child with her nose. "Come on, cub." He chirped and sluggishly got to his feet.

Dumpster gave a shrill note and ran up to Casseomae, clicking his incisors at her. "But what about my mischief? We can't leave the highway. I'll lose track of them."

Casseomae hated the thought of leaving the rat out here alone. He was tough and he'd come a long way already on his own, but she couldn't imagine that he'd survive for long.

"My responsibility is to the cub," she said grimly.

Dumpster sank back on his hind legs.

Casseomae figured there was danger any way they traveled. And Dumpster knew things about the cub and his kind that she never would have known otherwise. "Can we still follow the highway?" she asked the dog. "Will that lead to the Auspectres?"

"Yes, but like I said, it's a bad idea."

"But will it get us there?"

The dog looked over at the trembling rat. "It will."

"Then lead us that way," Casseomae said.

Dumpster snapped his tail in satisfaction and clambered onto her back more gently than before. As the dog set off down the highway, the cub slogged beside him, patting his head as they walked together. Casseomae was glad he liked the dog. She was glad to have another she could trust to protect her cub. He would need the dog if something were to ever happen to her.

They had only traveled until midday before the child slumped to the ground, whimpering and clutching his stomach. Casseomae lumbered over and licked his hand worriedly.

"What's wrong with him?" the dog asked, joining her.

"He hasn't eaten in a while," Casseomae said. "He needs food."

"There's food all around," the dog said. "I'll catch him a viand."

"He needs Old Devil food," Dumpster said. "His kind doesn't eat fresh kills."

"Sure they do," the dog argued.

"No, they don't." The rat clicked his teeth. "Only canned carcasses."

"Carcasses?" the dog replied with a bark. "I enjoy something dead and pungent on occasion, but I know the Companions don't. My ancestors hunted for them. We caught their meals, and they were fresh, not half-decayed."

"You don't know what you're talking about, cur," Dumpster said.

"Wait here. You'll see." The dog flitted off the highway and into the underbrush.

While Dumpster leaped down from Casseomae's back and began to rattle off the many reasons he despised dogs, Casseomae found a cane of ripe raspberries. She had nearly gotten her fill when the dog came back with a squirrel in his teeth, wagging his tail proudly. He dropped it before the child and gave a bark.

The child looked down at the limp squirrel at his feet and chirped something.

The dog panted cheerfully and said, "Go on. Try it."

"Watch, he isn't going to eat that," Dumpster said.

"You watch! Sure he will," the dog said. He picked the squirrel back up with his teeth and pressed it to the child. The boy pushed it away and stood.

"Let me show you," the dog said, putting his paws on the squirrel and tearing open its side with his jaws. "He just doesn't know how to get it open."

As the glistening pink-white organs spilled on the ground, the child put a hand to his mouth and backed away.

"Told you," the rat said, and moved off to search out some seeds and thistle to eat.

The dog looked from the child back to the squirrel with a perplexed cock to his head. "Maybe he just doesn't like squirrel." He dropped to his belly and began crunching into the squirrel. "No need to waste a good catch."

Casseomae returned to the berries. She hadn't been foraging long when she noticed the child watching her. His gaze flickered from the clusters of glistening berries to her. She understood his questioning look. She'd seen cubs look to their mothers this way. *Is it safe?*

She snorted in affirmation and continued eating, watching the child from the corners of her eyes. He plucked off a berry and sniffed it. He dabbed the berry to his tongue. A soft moan of pleasure came from the cub's throat, and he stuffed the berry in his mouth before reaching for more. Soon he was tearing the raspberries from the vines and eating them by the mouthful.

Casseomae swiveled her head around to the rat and dog. "Look!"

"Snip my tail!" Dumpster squeaked.

Casseomae rumbled with pleasure. The cub, her cub, was devouring a bear's feast in raspberries. Maybe there was other bear food he would eat. Maybe he just needed her to show him what was good. Wasn't that what a good mother was for?

The dog followed his nose over to a tree and gave a yip.

"What is it?" Casseomae asked.

"A scent marking," he said. "I think this is Gnash's territory."

"You know his pack?" Dumpster asked.

"I know them," the dog said, heading down the highway. "And the Ogeema holds sway over their pack. We'd better go."

CHAPTER EIGHTEEN

With food in his belly and his pouches bulging with berries, the child chased after the dog. None of them sensed wolves nearby, but Casseomae smelled their occasional markings and spied some of their droppings. She also came across rat droppings just after a section where the highway split. She let Dumpster down to investigate.

"Are they your mischief?"

"They sure are," Dumpster said happily before climbing back up.

By dark, they came to a creek dammed up into a pond over the highway by a family of beavers. Dumpster and the dog set off in opposite directions around the pond to hunt. Casseomae found some pickerelweed growing on the banks that she hoped the child would eat. The cub watched as she hooked a claw to the flower clusters and spilled out the fruit. After Casseomae ate some, the child picked up one of the fruits and tried it. The seed inside cracked under his teeth and he held his lips like he was going to spit it out. But then he gave a dog-smile and swallowed it, before eating more.

"I can't believe he's eating Forest food," Dumpster said as he returned. "He's either going to turn into a bear or fall over dead."

Casseomae snorted and foraged on water insects, leaving the child to crack open more of the pickerel-weed flowers. As darkness settled over the pond, the dog returned and flopped next to the child, who was searching for something in the pouch at his stomach.

"Is he really wearing a vora's hide?" the dog asked. "The wolves liked to taunt that the Companions only kept us around because they'd tear our hides off when they got cold. The pup looks like he's covered in some sort of hide, but I can't tell what vora it's from."

"It's from no vora nor viand," Dumpster said. "It's something the Old Devils made."

"That color," the dog said. "It's just like the sky. Just like his eyes."

"He fell from the sky," Casseomae said. "Maybe his hide and eyes are made of the sky."

"Doubtful," Dumpster said.

Casseomae scratched her itchy back against a rock. "But you don't know. You were wrong about what he ate."

"I wasn't wrong," Dumpster said. "The pup just has strange tastes. I still know a spittin' lot more than you, old bear." He snapped his tail. "Look at the pup over there. Either of you have any idea what he's holding in his hand?"

Casseomae rolled to her stomach to gaze at the child. He had out the flat piece of plastic he'd used to startle the cougar. She had come across objects like it on occasion. There were so many broken bits of relics around—in the Skinless's collapsed dens, strewn through the Forest, even sunk in the streambeds.

"Well, cur?" Dumpster asked. "He's your Companion. Any idea?"

The dog looked back at Dumpster, lapping his tongue. "No, what is it?"

"It's called a screen. It's an Old Devil device."

"What's a device?" the dog asked.

Dumpster sat back with a jaunty angle to his whiskers. "Something they made to do things. Some devices opened stuff and some made light. Other devices made noises and they used them to talk to others of their kind. That's sort of what a screen is."

"That screen isn't making any noises," Casseomae said.

"Maybe it's broken," Dumpster said. "I don't scratchin' know."

The dog panted a little laugh. "So you do admit, rat, there are some things you don't know."

"I never said I knew everything about the Old Devils," Dumpster said. "Just more than you beetle brains. And the name is Dumpster. She's Casseomae. What's yours anyway?"

"Pang," the dog replied.

"Cur name if I ever heard one," Dumpster muttered.

"Well, what kind of name is Dumpster?" Pang asked.

Dumpster considered the dog a moment before answering. "You ever been in any Old Devil cities?"

"Lots," Pang said.

"They've got these dumpsters the Old Devils kept beside their dens. It's where they put their best food and treasures. They'd make dumpsters out of metal. Huge heavy things. No cur or puss or even a bear for that matter could get into one." Dumpster paused to wiggle his whiskers. "But we did. Our ancestors got into their dumpsters. We snuck in and raided their precious caches and they couldn't stop us.

"It's a great honor to have my name," Dumpster said, continuing. "I'm the Memory for my mischief. Like a dumpster holds treasures, my memory holds the knowledge of the Old Devils. It's what's kept us alive. It's what's kept us from being wiped out by the voras."

"So your kind depended on the Companions—" Pang began.

Dumpster hissed so loudly and clicked his teeth so angrily that even the child looked up.

"Don't you say it. Don't you dare call my clan Faithful! We're not like you. We might have lived beneath their dens, but we stole from them. We never served them! We never promised to betray the clans of the Forest for those Devils!"

Pang flattened his ear. Without a word, he trotted around the pond and lay down with his snout on his paws. The child put the screen in his pouch and went after him.

Casseomae said, "I don't think the cub's screen is broken."

Dumpster was still eyeing the dog with irritable twitches of his whiskers. "Well, what do you reckon it's doing?"

"Have you heard how birds weave charms of leaves and twigs into their nests to protect their young?" she asked.

"I've heard they do that, but birds are superstitious pebble-brains."

Casseomae grunted. "The screen might be a piece of the sky. It might protect him."

Dumpster gave a dubious snort. "It wouldn't have saved him from that cougar."

"But it gave me the extra moment I needed to reach the cub in time. And maybe it was what led the cub to us. If the sky is the cub's true home, maybe the piece in his screen watches over him. It might have drawn us to him, so we could guard over him and keep him from harm."

"A piece of the sky," Dumpster scoffed. "You have some funny notions, birdbrain."

CHAPTER NINETEEN

Pang anxiously sniffed all morning as they journeyed. When they stopped in the shade of a crumbling overpass, he approached Casseomae. "I smell wolves. We need to leave the highway."

Dumpster shot toward him, trembling with fury. "But my mischief—"

A scent hit Casseomae's nose, and she reared up on her hind legs. The cub jumped to his feet in alarm and clutched her sides. The dog circled, looking around with his one ear alert. "What is it?"

Down the highway, from around a cluster of cars, a wolf appeared.

Dumpster leaped to Casseomae's back and scrambled up to her head, squeaking, "Go! Go!"

The child chirped wildly, but she nudged him into action. "Run, cub, before he calls his pack."

Pang led them from the highway, into the thick of the Forest, as the wolf's howl rang through the trees. "Where can we go?" she growled at the dog.

"I don't know," he said. "Just keep moving."

They tore through the underbrush and around trunks and saplings. "Is he following us?" Casseomae asked Dumpster.

"I don't see him." But no sooner had he said this than a series of barks answered the wolf's call. "That's a pack!" he squeaked, digging his claws into her scalp.

The child stumbled on a root and lay panting on the leaves, clutching his foot.

"Get up, cub," Casseomae said, nosing him under his ribs. She looked back anxiously. The wolves weren't yet in view, but they had their scent. It would only be moments before they arrived.

Casseomae dug her snout under the cub's frame until she forced him to his feet. "Listen, cub. I've got to carry you." She dropped flat and gestured with her nose toward her back.

The cub hesitated, then flung himself onto her back, grabbing at the thick folds of fat and fur around her throat. Casseomae sprang to her feet and dashed after the dog.

Pang flew over a log, gaining ground ahead of Casscomae. "I see something," he called.

A few strides more and Casseomae saw it too. A huge relic lay wedged between the trunks of some twisted maples.

"A passering," Dumpster said. "Get inside it!"

"But—" Casseomae began, knowing they'd only be trapped.

"Just do it," the rat ordered. "Before they see us."

The dog waited by the base of the relic. Casseomae passed him, bounding onto the wing. Dumpster leaped from her head and scampered through a broken window. The child slid from her back and tugged at the side of the passering. A crack appeared. Casseomae dug her claws around the edge and pried it open like a mussel shell.

The dog scrambled up onto the wing, his claws scrapping on the rust as he fled through the opening after the child. Once Casseomae was inside, the cub pulled the panel shut.

The light coming through the grimy windows was dim. "Is this what the pup came down in?" Pang asked, panting heavily on the mossy floor beside the child.

"No," Dumpster said. "This is an old one. Probably from before the Turning."

Barks grew louder and then Casseomae could hear the wolves surrounding the passering. "In there," one cried. "Look for a way in." A clattering of nails sounded on the wing outside followed by sniffs at the closed door.

The child clung to Casseomae's fur. A wolf scratched ferociously, trying to dig open the metal door. They couldn't open it, she was certain. Wolves couldn't use their forepaws like she and the cub could. But then a black nose wedged through the broken window where Dumpster had entered. Casseomae leaped up and raked her claws against it, sending the wolf whining back down the wing.

"Do you think they saw the pup?" Dumpster said as Casseomae settled back down.

"We're trapped in here either way," she replied. "This was a mistake, rat."

"You'd rather be out there?"

Casseomae growled.

"If the scout didn't see him," the dog said, "then they'll hopefully move on once they realize they can't reach us in here."

"And if they saw him?" Dumpster said.

"Just be quiet," Casseomae said, turning to comfort the trembling cub with licks.

The wolves growled and barked at one another, setting up a guard around the passering. Casseomae peered around the interior. The part she could see wasn't very wide, just enough for her to turn around. Up toward the nose, a dome of white leaned out from around a corner.

A skull. Most likely the carcass of the Skinless who had perished in the crash long ago. The cub clung tight to Casseomae's side and chirped softly to her.

Just when Casseomae thought the wolves might have left, she heard one up on the wing again, sniffing at the door. Once he had climbed back down, Dumpster ventured up to the broken window and peered out.

"Do you see them?" Casseomae asked.

"Yeah," the rat replied. "About ten. The way those underlickers are lounging around, they don't seem in any hurry to leave."

Casseomae dug her claws into the mildewed material lining the floor. She'd fight them, drive them off, but doing so would mean the cub would have to open the door. She couldn't risk his being seen. Besides, ten was a lot of wolves. She'd known male bears bigger than her taken down by that many. They waited and the setting sun sent golden shafts through the windows, and still the wolves kept the worrisome siege.

Dumpster sniffed. "Hey, there might be Old Devil food in here." He scampered up through the nooks lining the walls, and Pang rustled around to help, with the cub following him.

Casseomae lay listening for the wolves, but they were silent. "Any luck?"

"Nothing," Dumpster said, appearing from the shadows. "It's all been had by raccoons and mice."

The child returned, having found a metal stick, and settled back next to her, holding the stick tightly to his chest. When darkness finally began to fall and the cub lay sleeping against her side, Casseomae said, "We can't stay here forever."

Dumpster circled around her, his whiskers twitching. "I think I have an idea." Before she could ask what, the rat climbed up to the broken window and disappeared outside.

Casseomae exchanged a curious glance with Pang. She went to the window and peered out at the dark. All she could hear was the restless shifting of the wolves encamped around the passering. Where had that rat gone?

But then she heard wolves below, beneath the wing, talking to one another. ". . . his scout said it was protected by a bear."

"Is she the one?"

"The Ogeema will know when he arrives."

Casseomae jolted, feeling angry saliva fill her mouth. Was the Ogeema coming? She rounded to Pang, but before she could say anything, a wolf barked and then the whole growling pack was on their feet, their paws crunching on leaves. An odor crept through the broken window, a noxious and eye-stinging vapor. The cub woke and whimpered to Casseomae.

"I don't know, little cub," she said, licking him. "But stay quiet."

Her nose ran violently, and Pang seemed to be suffering the same result, because he shook his head trying to drive the terrible smell away. "What's that rat done?" he whined.

Dumpster came back through the window. "I think it's working," he said gleefully.

"What is?" Casseomae growled.

"Listen," the rat replied, sitting on his haunches.

The wolves barked at one another, but Casseomae could hear their steps moving back from the passering.

"Gasoline," Dumpster said. "Fortunately it hadn't leaked from the crash. I snipped a line and let it spill out. An old mischief trick my da taught me."

Casseomae stood up to peer through the window. The wolves were retreating. She felt her head swimming and said, "Have you poisoned us to keep the wolves from having the cub?"

"It's not so strong in here," Dumpster said.

"It's strong enough to make my tongue feel like pine bark," Pang complained.

"Oh, shut it, cur," he said. "The effects will pass. But I spilled it right on some of those idiot wolves. They'll have a time getting that stink from their noses, not to mention trying to scratchin' follow us now."

Casseomae heard the wolves call to one another, the sounds growing distant. The cub was burying his face in her fur. "We need to leave," she said. "I heard the wolves say that the Ogeema was coming."

"What?" Pang snapped. "You must have heard wrong."

"I didn't."

"This is Gnash's realm," Pang said. "The Ogeema might hold sway over other pack chiefs, but he'd never enter another pack's territory."

Casseomae growled up at Dumpster peering through the window. "Can we go?"

"All right, then." He slipped through the broken glass.

Casseomae pushed against the door and it creaked open. Pang dashed out first, and as soon as he stopped on the wing, he whined, "Blessed Companions, it's worse out here!"

"Just watch out you don't step in it," Dumpster said from the edge of the wing. "It's mostly under the passering, so just get all the way down here before you hop off."

Casseomae's snout burned as she came out. She couldn't smell anything besides the awful poisons Dumpster had released. She listened for the wolves, hearing only distant howls.

"Come on, cub," she called back. "Stay close."

The child emerged from the doorway looking around warily. He poked his metal stick out at the dark Forest and made a *pop* with his lips.

The four hurried from the passering without getting any of the smell on their paws, and after they had traveled a time, Casseomae felt her head clearing.

"That was pretty clever," she admitted to Dumpster.

He leaped onto her forepaw and climbed up to settle at the back of her head. "Of course it was," he said. "I'm a rat, after all."

CHAPTER TWENTY

Casseomae worried as they journeyed along a rolling stretch of the Forest the next morning. Could the Ogeema himself really be searching for the cub?

Pang gauged their direction with the rising sun. When he stopped abruptly, Casseomae felt her legs tighten, ready for battle. The cub, paying more attention now to the reactions of the other three, knelt and pointed his metal stick out protectively.

"What is it?" Casseomae said. "I don't smell wolves."

"Not wolves," Pang said, looking around. A long line of ruined buildings stretched in either direction along a narrow trail. Several of the buildings had tall colorful treelike billboards and signs of plastic and metal rising from the ground. "I recognize this place."

"Scratchin' good for you," Dumpster said. "Now can we keep moving?"

Pang trotted over to Casseomae. "We're getting near the Auspectres."

Casseomae looked around at the ruins. "The witches live here?"

"No," Pang said. "But we need something first."

"What's that?" she asked.

"We need to bring them a carcass," Pang said.

"Oh, I see how this works," Dumpster said, leaping down from Casseomae. "Very clever. They convince voras to bring them their catch rather than having to search the Forest for it. Got to admire their knack for taking advantage of the gullible."

"It's not for food," Pang said. "They divine the future from the carcass."

"You're saying they don't eat it?" Dumpster asked.

"Of course they do, but if we don't bring them a carcass, they'll have nothing to use to answer our question."

"Well, it won't be a problem," Casseomae said. "There are kills all over the Forest. I smell some rotting elk nearby at this very moment."

"It's not that simple," Pang said. "We can't just bring them the first pile of maggoty hide and bones we find. It's got to be something good. Something fresh. Otherwise, they might require an offering as well."

Dumpster rose on his hind legs. "What do you mean, 'an offering'?"

"They require payment. If the carcass is good enough, they might need nothing extra. But if it's not, you might have to give something else. It really depends on the question and how difficult it is to divine."

"Was yours difficult?" Casseomae asked.

"Yes."

"And what did you bring them?"

"A pair of rabbits. It was a fresh kill. I thought they would like that. But there are so many of them. . . ." He shivered. "A pair of rabbits was hardly enough to go around. To answer my question, they told me I had to give them something else."

"Another catch?" Casseomae asked.

"No."

"What, then?"

Pang dropped his snout, his lone ear twitching. "My ear. They took my ear as a sacrifice for the knowledge that would eventually save my life."

Casseomae looked at the gaping ear hole on the side of Pang's head and the scars around it.

"How big a viand can you carry?" Pang asked. "Could you carry a doe?"

"Yes, something bigger even, I'd suppose."

"Good," Pang said. "We're going to try a tactic my pack used. Come on."

The trail met up with a line of buildings. The ruined dens went on and on, occasionally spreading out to the sides where other trails intersected the main one. Casseomae hadn't seen so many buildings before, and she asked Dumpster, "Is this a city?"

"No," the rat laughed. "Not like the city where I'm from. The dens go up and up. But this was some sort of colony."

"All the rock the Companions placed for trails keeps the trees from growing thick here," Pang said. "Good foraging for the viands. Lots of drinking holes too. When the sun sets, the tribes of deer will come in from the Forest. We just need to find . . . yes, I think I see something."

The dog sprinted ahead with the child chasing after him. The two reached a jumble of cars that made a wall across the road. They climbed over and disappeared on the other side. When Casseomae and Dumpster clambered over a car's hood, Pang was investigating a building that had crumbled into a cove of rock and metal.

"Look over there," Dumpster said. "Those are dumpsters!"

Casseomae eyed the big metal containers as Pang trotted back.

"This will do," he said. "So you know how when you're running down a herd of deer, you hope to catch the slowest. A fawn or an old buck or an injured doe."

Pang looked around. "But sometimes, you can trap them. If they panic and run into this den . . ."

"Not bad," Dumpster said.

"You'll stay here," Pang said to Casseomae. "Hide on the other side of those relics where they won't smell you. I'll go down a ways and find a water hole. I'll wait there. When the deer arrive, I'll drive them this way. You'll steer them into that den. Then we can get a big one."

"You don't have a pack to help you," Casseomae said. "You expect to be able to scare them all?"

"I can manage," Pang said. "I could take the pup with me. He could help."

"No," Casseomae said. "I'm not letting him out of my sight."

Dumpster let out a squeak of amusement. "Nice try, cur. Want to live out your hunting fantasies with a real Companion?"

Pang gave an affronted lift of his snout. "Just be ready," he said before trotting away.

The child began to follow him, but Casseomae gave a gruff bark. He looked back at her. She lumbered toward him, nipping gently at his elbow. "Come back here with me."

The child watched Pang disappear. His shoulders slumped and he chirped something softly under his breath.

As the sun set and they waited, Dumpster slunk around the undersides of the cars, scaring up grasshoppers from the weeds and catching them in his sharp teeth. The child watched with delight. When a grasshopper landed near his leg, the child crouched over it with cupped hands. With a quick grab, he caught it. He let out a laugh and ran over toward Dumpster.

The rat scampered behind Casseomae. "I'll catch them myself," he sniffed.

Casseomae lay on her stomach, chewing on soft shoots. The child looked at her, the grasshopper pinched between his fingers. Slowly he approached, holding out the insect.

She knew what he wanted to do and gave a gentle huff. When he extended his hand toward her snout, she reached out with her long lips and took it from his fingers.

The cub stood back up, a wide grin on his face.

"You're a weird one, Cass," Dumpster said.

The cub ran off to catch another grasshopper, but when he brought it to her, she turned her head away. It had been funny the first time. A curiosity. To let her cub feed her. But it wasn't right. He had to catch food for himself.

He pushed the grasshopper to her lips, his eyes wide with eagerness. But she grunted, "No," and lowered her head to bite another cluster of grass.

The child looked at the grasshopper in his fingers. He watched it for a moment and then stuck it in his mouth, crunching on the body with a wrinkled nose. When he at last swallowed it, he looked around and set off to catch another.

Dumpster flicked his tail. "Weird," he said. "Just scratchin' weird."

The sun sank over the buildings, turning the sky crimson-pink. Casseomae looked over the car's hood but didn't spy Pang. Rabbits were hopping slowly among the weeds, their eyes and ears cautious for approaching voras, but they clearly couldn't smell her. That was good.

She paced around behind the wall of cars while the child sat nearby, poking a tire with the wide end of his metal stick. As usual, Dumpster had crawled under something to nap.

A bark erupted. Casseomae peered over the hood and spied Pang's copper-red coat flashing down the trail.

Ahead of him were several deer—a buck with wide antlers, a few does, and a fawn—leaping this way and that, wide-eyed with fear and searching for some way to escape through the maze of cars. The does stayed close to the fawn, protectively. The buck's gaze fell on the wall of cars blocking his path. He snorted something back at the does in his tribe's tongue.

He was about to leap over the wall when Casseomae

rose up on a car. The buck froze, throwing his head side to side. There was nowhere left to go but into the neighboring building. Casseomae hoped Pang had made sure there weren't any escape holes back in the dark corners.

With Pang snapping at their tails, the does and the fawn dashed past the buck into the building. The buck snorted before following.

"We've got them!" Pang barked.

Casseomae dug her claws into the car's rusty metal and bounded to the other side. The shadows of the building had deepened, and it took her a moment to find the deer frozen in a cluster at the far end, heads snapped up, snorting and stamping with fear.

Pang and Casseomae spread out, blocking the way back out. The buck stepped forward to defend the herd. It lowered its antlers at Pang.

"He might try to go for you," Casseomae warned.

The dog curled his lips. He snapped savagely. The buck stepped back, tipping and raising his antlers in warning.

Casseomae slowly approached. Which one should she take? Not the fawn. She wasn't above eating a fawn. She had done it plenty. It was the way of the Forest. But a fawn might not be good enough for the Auspectres. She needed a doe.

Pang edged around to cut the buck off from the others. He snapped at his legs, and the buck drove him back with a stab of his antlers, nearly spearing Pang's side.

A cry came behind them. Casseomae turned to see the cub. He had climbed over the cars, his teeth bared like the dog's. He jabbed the stick and cried out again in a little roar.

A blur of brown swished around Casseomae, the does and the fawn using the moment to get past her. Casseomae raced after them, but knew she was too late. They rounded the corner of the building, white tails flashing, and escaped back down the trail from where they had come.

Pang was ferociously barking, and as Casseomae spun around once more, she saw the buck getting away. He couldn't follow the other deer—Casseomae had his path blocked. There was only one way to go. Over the wall of cars.

And standing between the buck and his escape was her cub.

CHAPTER TWENTY-ONE

The child panicked as the buck raced toward him. He stumbled backward, banging into the car and shrinking down.

The buck's hooves clattered on the concrete, and he dipped his antlers. The cub pointed the stick at the buck and turned his head away. Casseomae roared as the deer leaped, taking flight.

A thunderclap of noise erupted, and a lightning streak of fire flashed from the front of the stick. The buck fell, toppling to the top of the car just above the child's head. The boom echoed away through the trees.

The cub stared down wide-eyed at the smoking stick in his hand. He staggered to his feet and looked at the deer lying on the car. The buck was dead. Blood ran down the rusted metal from beneath his body. The child threw down the stick, whimpering.

"What just happened?" Casseomae growled.

Pang circled around the dropped stick, sniffing at it anxiously. "It . . . it came from that! How did he do that?"

Dumpster scuttled from under the car and approached the stick. He looked from it to the deer and then at the child. "Did the cub scratchin' kill it?"

"Yes, but how—?" Casseomae began.

"It's a gun," the rat squeaked. "It has to be. I've heard of these Old Devil weapons."

"Didn't you recognize it when he was carrying it?" she asked.

"He's picked up so many things," the rat said. "And these guns, I knew of them and I've seen a few, but they were huge and mounted to vehicles. I've never seen one this small."

The child stared in shock at the deer. Water trickled from his eyes and he began shaking uncontrollably.

"It's all right, pup," Pang said, licking his trembling fingers. He turned excitedly to Casseomae. "He's a real vora! The pup . . . he's a hunter now. Can you believe it? He can—" But then he stopped as a fierce note of disapproval rose from Casseomae's throat.

She nudged the child with her wet nose. "It's safe, cub." The child threw his arms around her neck and buried his face. She licked his ears, trying to calm him.

"We should go," Dumpster said. "The smell of the carcass will draw attention. Not to mention that ear-shattering noise."

Casseomae eased away from the cub and loped over to take the buck's throat in a firm grip. She pulled him from the car. The child wiped the wetness from his face, still trembling. He followed Casseomae as she dragged the heavy animal.

Pang looked back at the gun and barked, "He should take it. We might need a weapon like that."

Dumpster gave Casseomae a disconcerted look. The child hurried away from Pang and the weapon lying in the road. "Come on, cub," she grunted through her teeth, which were locked on the deer.

Pang lingered a moment by the gun and gave a whine before trotting ahead of the others to lead the way.

CHAPTER TWENTY-TWO

The Forest had fewer trees, just spindly pines jabbing up through the scrub and concrete. Pang sniffed noisily as they went. Casseomae had smelled no territory markings, smelled no signs of any vora, which seemed odd.

"Who rules this domain?" she asked through teeth clenched on the deer.

"The Auspectres," the dog said. "Well, they don't exactly rule it. It's more that no one else wants to live near them. You'll see why. And don't let down your guard. Voras still pass through these hills."

Casseomae brushed her side against the cub, reminding him to stay close. He stroked her fur gently.

The land rose steeply. Dusk became night. Casseomae grew tired of dragging the heavy buck across the rocky terrain. As they reached the crest of a hill, Pang stopped. "There!"

Silhouetted against the bone-white moon and the misty horizon was what appeared to Casseomae to be an enormous tree rising from the next hill. But it couldn't be a tree. It was too massive, too angular and evenly shaped.

"Is that an electricity tower?" Dumpster asked. "I can't believe it's still standing."

Pang lifted his ear. "What's a lick-trick city tower?"

"Electricity," the rat answered. "Like what's in lightning. It's how the Old Devils made their devices work. They built these towers to steal electricity from storms. But I thought for sure these towers all fell."

"Is that where we'll find the Auspectres?" Casseomae asked.

"Don't you see them?" asked Pang.

Casseomae looked again. She realized that what she first took to be foliage covering the tree were in fact vultures, moving and shifting in place. She'd never seen so many in one place.

Although she hadn't heard of vultures attacking voras, their sheer number put her on edge. If for some reason they did attack, they would be overwhelmed.

Casseomae dropped the deer. "Maybe you all should stay here," she said.

"Good idea," Dumpster said before slipping under some brush.

Pang woofed at the cub, "Stay with me."

The child looked questioningly at Casseomae. She nuzzled him with her snout and snorted, "It's safe, cub."

He let out a noise she had never heard before, something between a bark and a whine. It startled her.

"It almost sounded like Vorago, didn't it?" Dumpster said. "Almost like 'don't go.'"

Pang also had a look of disbelief on his face, his lone ear stuck straight up. Then he shook his coat and butted against the child. "She'll be back," Pang assured him with a lick.

Casseomae carried the deer toward the tower. As she made her way up the slope, she passed carcasses littering the ground. They were mostly bones, occasionally emerging from stiff peeled-back hides. Most were viands—turkeys, squirrels, woodchucks, and deer, although none as large as Casseomae's buck. But there were voras, too. Curs mainly, but also coyotes, bobcats, and foxes. And one carcass Casseomae felt certain was a wolf. She could hardly imagine what creature other than another wolf would have brought this offering.

Swarms of flies rose in the air, their droning filling her ears. The sweet odor of rot was overwhelming. Coming from the base of the tower was a stronger smell, something acidic that she knew to be mounds of droppings. The smells stung her senses and made her feel dizzy and vulnerable.

She glanced up to see, one by one, vultures taking flight. They circled on long black wings and slowly descended. Casseomae let go of the deer and backed away in case a battle broke out over the carcass.

But as the vultures landed, they kept their distance from Casseomae and her offering. More and more of the birds swept down, until they surrounded her in a flapping mass of oily black. Their heads and necks were featherless, their cinder-colored skin deeply wrinkled. They cast their heads side to side, peering at Casseomae with blood-brown eyes.

She had always thought vultures had no speech, since she'd never heard them call with the melodic songs that other birds used. But low hisses began, terrible threatening-sounding gasps that rose and fell. Soon words emerged from the hisses, although Casseomae could not tell which of the black witches was speaking.

"A good offering," they hissed in Vorago. "A good offering, yes, for our sisters. She has come seeking an answer, hasn't she? Yes, she has a need. She desires our guidance. We will ask the dead. Yes, they know. They always know."

The words swirled around Casseomae, whispers blown past her ears. The vultures were a black fog of feathers and hooked beaks and scarred heads. Casseomae found them gruesome and wanted nothing more than to be away from the filthy carrion eaters.

"The Forest lives off of death," they hissed as if sensing her thoughts. "Without death there would be no life. She finds us hideous! Frightening. But the Forest would not survive without us. We draw life from the dead. And for you, yes, for you, bear, we will draw answers from the dead. He will tell us what is to come. So what is it you want to know?"

Casseomae turned, looking for which vulture to address. "My cub," she said before circling to the ones behind her. "My cub is being hunted. By the wolves. I fear the Ogeema is coming for him. I need to know where I can take him that will be safe."

The vultures grunted and hissed as they looked around at each other. "A bear's cub? Why would the Ogeema spare a step following a bear's little cub? It makes no sense, does it, sisters?"

"You must believe me," Casseomae said. "I've brought you this buck. You've said it's a good offering. Tell me where my cub will be safe."

The circle of vultures grew more animated, pecking and beating their wings against one another. "Where is your cub now?"

"Nearby," she said. "Hiding."

"Bring the cub to us," they hissed.

"No! Something else," Casseomae growled. "I am willing to give you a sacrifice. You can take my ear, but you can't have the cub."

"We don't want your cub, mother bear. But in order to know where your cub will be safe, we need to see him."

Casseomae paced nervously. She had no idea how the vultures felt about the Skinless Ones. Had their kind been subject to cruelties before the Turning?

"All right," she said. "I'll bring him to you. But you promise you won't harm him?"

"We bring life, mother bear. We do not take it. Your cub will be safe from us."

The vultures parted to allow Casseomae through. She loped down the hill feeling anxious.

Pang sat up from the grass when she reached them. "What is it?" the dog asked. "Did they tell you?"

"No. They want to see the cub."

Dumpster emerged from the shadows. "You're not going to show him to those witches?"

"What else can I do?" she snorted fearfully. "They'll not answer the question otherwise. What do you think, dog? Can I trust the Auspectres?"

Pang's remaining ear flicked several times. "Yes, I believe you can trust them."

She grunted at the cub. "Come."

He sprang to his feet and ran to her side. As she turned to lumber back up the hill, the cub held a hand to her shoulder. "It will be fine, cub. You'll be safe with me. Stay close."

As they neared the vultures, the huge birds reared their wings, spitting and hissing and sputtering. Casseomae slowed, pacing forward cautiously until she and the child were in the center of them.

The hisses grew into words, swirling out from their hooked beaks. "You did not tell us. You lied! This is not your cub. This is not yours."

"Yes, he is," Casseomae growled.

The child shrank down, trembling against Casseomae with his hands over his face.

"He is my cub," she said, licking him. "And I will do anything to protect him from the wolves."

The hisses quieted until only the buzz of flies filled the night air. It disturbed Casseomae to see so many tall creatures around her and for them to be so silent. They held their crooked wings aloft and swayed their wrinkled black heads.

"I know it is different now," Casseomae said. "Now that you see what my cub is. Now you understand why the wolves want him. If the buck is not enough, if you need something else, some other offering to help find the answer . . ."

"No," a vulture whispered.

Casseomae snapped her head toward the vulture who had spoken. But it was another who answered. "You need make no other sacrifice, mother bear. This cub, he will pay us—"

Casseomae lunged with a growl. "You said you would not harm him!"

The vultures did not flinch. "He will bring death," one said.

"Lots of death to the Forest," added another.

"From this death will rise new life."

"He will make an offering to us in this way."

Casseomae looked around. "Then tell me where I must go."

The vultures tucked their wings and bobbed their heads and began their chorus of hissing. Three of their flock hopped forward to the buck. Their hooked beaks cut through the hide.

The child whimpered, and Casseomae grunted gently, "Hush now."

The three pulled apart the deer's belly, dragging out his entrails. But they did not eat them. Once the bloody viscera were scattered before their talons, the three vultures drew back to join their sisters. They whispered to one another.

"Can you tell?" Casseomae asked.

"We can tell," they said. "We see where you must take him. He will be safe. If you can only get him there."

"Where is it?" she asked. "Where do I take him?"

"The Island of the Sun," they answered. "Where it rises from the Wide Waters."

"I've never been to the Wide Waters."

"He will lead you," they hissed. "The cub's companion will show you how to find it. We smell him nearby. He came to us before. Yes, he did, sisters. When he and his pack were being hunted like your cub. He will lead you to the island."

"An island?" she asked. "How do we reach it? Do we have to swim?"

"No. You will walk. To reach the Island of the Sun, you must walk over the water."

"A bridge?" Casseomae growled. Most of the bridges they'd encountered had crumbled ages ago.

"You will know where you must cross when you have reached the place at the shore that is a territory of viands."

"A territory of viands...," she said. "Do you mean... Is it the Havenlands?"

"We have heard it called that. Yes, we have. And we have seen this place. It is our small cousins who have named it the Havenlands. But you cannot stay there. For the cub to be safe you must pass through the Havenlands and go over the water to the Island of the Sun.

"The cub's companion," they hissed. "He will know how to lead you there. Tell him to ascend a great height. From there you will see the spinning trees that mark the Havenlands. When he sees, he will know where to go."

The vultures began closing in around them. The

child murmured in fright. Casseomae backed away with the cub close to her side.

"We have told you," they hissed. "And you must go. A good offering. A good offering you have given us. And more to come if you are successful."

Casseomae backed farther until she was out from the ring of vultures. The vultures spat and pecked at one another as they swarmed over the buck and tore it apart.

"Come, cub," she said. But he was already gone, racing back toward Pang.

CHAPTER TWENTY-THREE

The child was stumbling with tiredness, but Casseomae would not stop until they were far from the Auspectres' tower.

"Me?" Pang said. "They said I would be able to lead you to this island?"

"They said to tell you to ascend a great height," Casseomae said grimly, "so you could see the spinning trees that mark the Havenlands."

"Spinning trees. Havenlands. Climbing into the sky." Dumpster slapped his tail scornfully. "Scratchin' mites! I knew this was a waste of time."

Pang tucked his tail with a whine.

The rat circled around in agitation before saying, "Unless . . ."

"Unless what?" Casseomae grunted.

"If we could get to the top of a skyscraper—assuming there's one left standing—we could see a far distance from up there. Pang, is there a city nearby?"

The dog lifted his head. "Yes, several days' journey toward Sun's Birth."

"Then lead us there," Casseomae said.

Pang looked at the cub. "I don't go into cities if I can help it. And this city . . . I've only skirted its borders. I hear there are strange tribes living there. Creatures seen nowhere else in the Forest. I hardly know if they are vora or viand."

"It won't matter," Casseomae said. "We're not letting any of them catch a sniff of the cub. We'll travel quietly."

"Yes, old bear," Dumpster said. "You and that cub of yours are nothing if not a stink blossom of stealth. Oh, a city!" he squeaked excitedly. "Now we're scratchin'. I'm so sick of all these trees and endless walking and bear riding. A nice city sounds right up my alley."

"What's an alley?" Pang asked.

"It's a . . . ah, never mind," the rat sighed, settling happily atop Casseomae's head.

The following day brought them into territory rich for foraging. The child discovered a black cherry tree, heavy with small fruits, and filled his mouth and pockets with the juicy cherries. But a faint smell caused Casseomae to growl at the others to be quiet.

Distant howls echoed through the Forest.

"Can you tell if they're after us?" she asked Pang.

"The wolves in this territory don't pay tribute to the Ogeema," the dog said. "Those are hunting cries. They're chasing something. A deer most likely. Which means they're not onto us. They wouldn't be so loud if they were."

"Maybe," Dumpster said. "Do you know these underlickers?"

"It's Maul's pack, I think. A vicious ruler," Pang said, looking back toward the fading sounds of the hunt. "I wish we'd never let the cub leave that weapon behind."

They passed over many stands of fine foraging for the sake of covering ground. The child ate the last of his cherries as the sun was dipping low through the trees.

They had come upon a wide river with more of the Skinless Ones' dens lining its banks when the child knelt to the ground with a hand to his stomach. He let out a moan and then a sharp cry as he doubled over.

Pang ran up to lick his face. "What's wrong, pup?"

Casseomae sniffed, trying to tell if something had bitten him.

All at once, the child vomited and toppled to one side. He continued to retch as he lay shaking on the ground.

Pang barked, "Get up! Get up! What's the matter?"

Casseomae pushed her snout under the cub to roll

him over. He was caked in the sick and was limp, his eyes flickering.

"If he spit up, he ought to feel better," she growled fearfully. "What's happened to him?"

"He was eating Forest food," Pang said. "I told you he shouldn't eat Forest food! Maybe he ate a mushroom when we weren't watching. Some of those are poisonous. Or a toad? I've seen pack mates go dizzy for hours after eating a bad toad."

Casseomae sniffed the contents of the vomit on the ground. It was no different than anything she'd eaten.

Dumpster was scampering around, trying to stay clear of the dog's and bear's anxious paws. "I think I know," he said. "It's part of the Memory."

"What?" Casseomae said. "What's happened?"

"The pup . . . it's like what happened to all the other Old Devils," Dumpster said. "Back before the Turning. The pup, I think he's got the sickness. I . . . I think he's dying."

"What?" Casseomae growled. She sniffed at the cub anxiously. He was no longer vomiting, but his eyes were shut and his breath sounded raspy.

"I'm trying to remember," he said. "There're so many stories. But have you heard why the Old Devils are no longer here?"

"A cowardly trick," Pang said. "The Ogeema's ancestor Taka-Dirge disguised himself as a dog and snuck into the den of the great Companion chiefs. He let the armies of wolves in and they killed the Companion chiefs in their sleep—"

"Cur nonsense," Dumpster said, sitting back on his haunches. "Nobody really knows for sure how the Old Devils vanished. You ask the birds and they'll tell you they were burned up in the sun because they flew too high in their passerings. I've heard the pusses say their old masters ran out of food and all starved or killed one another fighting over scraps. But that isn't what my da told me. That's not what the Memory holds. No, the Memory for our mischief tells that the Old Devils got sick. Suddenly. All of them at once."

"Couldn't they just eat mallow or grass or something?" Pang asked. "That's what helps when we get sick."

"The Old Devils had food like that," Dumpster replied. "They called them medicines. But this sickness killed them all before they could figure out which medicines to eat."

"But if that's what happened, then what about the pup and the others of his kind who came down from the sky?" Casseomae asked.

"I don't know." Dumpster flattened his whiskers. "I'm just telling you the Memory."

"Maybe some of the Companions flew off in a passering before they got sick," Pang suggested. "They could have done that."

"And what?" Dumpster scoffed. "They've been living up in that passering for all this time? What would they eat?"

The child groaned and Casseomae nudged him soothingly with her nose. "Is there nothing we can do? I can't just let him die."

"Maybe the rat's wrong," Pang said, trying to reassure her.

Dumpster clicked his teeth. "Not scratchin' likely!"

Pang snarled. "Shut up, you idiot. Can't you see she's upset?" He eyed the growing purple and pink twilight sky. "It will be dark soon."

"The pup can't stay out here," Dumpster said. "That spew smell on him will draw night voras. We need to get him underground . . . or at least somewhere you can defend him better."

"What about that Companion den up there?" Pang said. "It's not so ruined."

Casseomae eyed the wooden building. It was covered in creeper and a fallen oak lay on a portion of the roof, but for the most part it was intact. "It'll do."

She picked the cub up at the shoulder, as she'd done the day she'd first rescued him. With a gentle grip of her teeth, she carried him toward the building. Pang ran ahead, sniffing for signs of danger as they went inside.

"Not there in the glass," Dumpster squeaked. "Over here." He directed her toward a back corner.

After she put the child down, Casseomae surveyed the den. Unlike her den back in the meadow, the floor was the smooth flat sort of wood that the Skinless fashioned. On the far end of the den where the oak had landed, the building was in ruins with weeds and saplings rising through the rotten floor. But on this side, it was dry and mostly well-preserved.

"It's even got furniture," Dumpster said, sniffing around with interest.

"What's fern-of-chirp?" Pang asked.

"Furniture, you idiot. That stuff over there. It's nesting the Old Devils used to keep their pups off the ground. They believed the earth was cursed and to touch it would defile you. That's why they built their skyscraper dens so high."

"How's the pup?" Pang said, circling back to Casseomae.

She was trying to lick the sick from his clothing hide, but it had soaked into the material. "He seems to be sleeping," she replied. She got the worst of it off, but he still smelled strongly.

As evening fell, they heard scurrying in the rafters above. An opossum poked its head curiously through a hole in the ceiling and Dumpster said, "What are you looking at?" He disappeared, but Casseomae knew the den must house any number of viand families like squirrels and birds and even some smaller voras like raccoons.

"You might not want to wander much, rat," she cautioned.

"Eh," Dumpster said dismissively, but he settled onto the arm of a couch close by.

Pang nervously watched the woods from the doorway. Casseomae was glad to have him standing guard. She continued to soothe the cub, slicking back the tuft of hair on his head with her long tongue.

A painful memory dredged itself up. Not many moons before, she had been licking a pair of tiny cubs she had given birth to over the winter. They had arrived breathless, like all the other cubs she'd borne. Sick with anger and desperation, she had licked the cubs all through the frosty night, hoping that somehow she could bring them to life.

"Don't leave me, cub," she whispered to the child as she drew her tongue over his thick ears. His skin was salty and hot. "You're strong. You're not like other cubs. And you're stronger than the others of your kind. You survived when they haven't. Please, just get better."

His eyes didn't open. But the child murmured and brushed a hand to her snout, weakly trying to push her away. "Good," she said, feeling a stirring in her chest. "Sleep. Just sleep."

Later an eruption of distant barks broke the quiet of the night. Pang leaped up from the doorway. "Do you hear that?" he barked. "Those are wolves."

"How far away?" Dumpster asked.

"Not far enough," Pang said.

Casseomae rose and stepped out into the night air. The barks grew rapid and ferocious. "What are they doing?" she called back to Pang.

"Those aren't howls to mark territory." He listened as the faint cries continued. "I think those are wolves fighting other wolves."

"That's a lot of wolves," Dumpster said.

Casseomae went out to stand on her hind legs. She couldn't smell them, which was good. They were still a fair distance away. But if those wolves came near, they would certainly be caught. She hurried back inside to find Pang tugging at the child. "What are you doing?"

Pang had torn a portion of the cub's blue clothing away from his chest and was chewing at the portions around his waist. The child whimpered and curled up but didn't open his eyes.

"He's getting that reeking coat off of him!" Dumpster said.

"Stop," Casseomae growled, butting the dog in the ribs.

Pang looked up with urgent eyes. "The smell. We'll never get it cleaned off that strange hide. It's not like fur and if we don't get it out of here, they'll smell the pup."

"The cur's right," Dumpster said. "We've got to get rid of that."

Casseomae lumbered to the child's face and licked him soothingly while Pang continued to gnaw and tear away the rest of the clothing hide. Underneath the cub wore another smaller white covering around his midsection. Pang left it along with the thick coverings on the child's feet since neither had gotten any vomit on them. Once the remains of the child's clothing hide lay on the floor, Pang gathered it up in his teeth and carried it out the doorway.

"Leaving it out there won't do any scratchin' good," Dumpster called.

Pang dropped it and barked, "I'm taking it to the river," before trotting off with the reeking hide in his mouth.

Casseomae turned back to the child, curled up like a pink newborn, looking more vulnerable than ever. He shivered even though the night was warm. She lay against him, settling his whimpers with licks. Soon the cub relaxed into quiet sleep.

When Pang returned, he said, "It's stopped."

Casseomae lifted her head to listen. The noise of the fighting wolves had gone quiet.

CHAPTER TWENTY-FOUR

Casseomae slept little that night. Her ears were attuned to every noise. Whenever Pang sat up in the doorway, she growled, "Are they here?"

"No," he'd say before sniffing cautiously and then setting his chin back on his paws.

Eventually she did doze, and when the child began stirring in the morning, she woke to find him curled up against her stomach. She gave him a lick and the cub opened his eyes. He sat up with a start and then touched a hand to her fur.

If he was surprised that his clothing hide was gone, he didn't show it. He stood and took a few wobbly steps over to Pang. The dog lapped at his hands with a grin. "He looks better."

Casseomae agreed. "He does."

Dumpster crawled out and twitched his whiskers at the child. "I can't scratchin' believe it. Thought for sure he was one for the crows."

Casseomae's fur tingled with happiness. She brushed up against the cub. He staggered but gave a weak grin before going to the door.

"Let's hope he can travel soon," Pang said as he followed him outside.

Dumpster and Pang searched the tall weeds around the house for insects, while Casseomae foraged for leaves and chokeberries. The cub didn't eat, and she worried what he'd do without his drinking device until she found him sipping river water from his hands.

The strange coverings on the cub's feet made the legs protruding from their tops look all the skinnier. Casseomae gave a snort as she watched him wading out into the river to splash water on his face and chest. "He looks like a frog," she said.

"Palest frog I've ever seen." Pang grinned.

Dumpster gave a squeak. "Look at this! What are these in his spew?"

Casseomae lumbered to where the rat was sniffing at the dried pile of sick in the grass.

"See those seeds?" Dumpster said.

Pang pulled his nose back. "Smells like centipedes."

"Centipedes?" the rat squeaked. "The pup wasn't eating spittin' centipedes."

But Casseomae caught the scent. The dog was right. There were certain large black and yellow centipedes she'd tried to eat that released a poison from their backs. The smell was unmistakably the same.

"Those seeds are from the cherries," she grunted. "I ate them and they didn't bother me."

"You're not an Old Devil," Dumpster said.

Casseomae gave him a snort. "You think they're what poisoned the cub? He wasn't coming down with the sickness that wiped his kind out?"

"Hopefully," the rat said.

Casseomae grunted and looked for the child. He'd found a portion of his clothing hide in the river and was dragging it up on shore.

"No," Pang barked, running over to pull it away from him.

The child chirped irritably at the dog and held on to the blue hide. Something fell to the ground and the child quickly let go of the clothing to grab it.

"It's the screen," Casseomae said.

The child ran to huddle behind Casseomae to keep the dog from taking the screen.

"Let him have it," she huffed.

The child huddled over the device, punching his fingers at it. The blue light they'd seen before didn't illuminate and the child grumbled angrily at Pang.

"What's he saying?" Pang asked.

"He's your Companion," Dumpster said. "If you plan on taking up with his kind again, you'd better learn his tongue."

Pang wagged his tail and panted, trying to cheer the cub up. But the child simply shook water from the seam of the device, ignoring the dog. He put his arms around Casseomae's neck and slumped onto her back. Casseomae gave Pang a warning look before lumbering off.

"What's the matter with them?" Pang said to Dumpster. "I didn't do anything."

Dumpster flicked his whiskers. "She thinks the screen's a piece of the sky. She thinks it was protecting the pup."

"I didn't know!" Pang said. "I was just trying to help the pup. Is it true? Was it protecting him?"

Dumpster scampered after Casseomae without answering. Pang tucked his tail between his legs and trotted after them. They followed the river, which Pang said flowed to the city, until midday. The child got down sluggishly, still weak from the sickness. But when Casseomae dug up some bulbs from the water's edge to eat, he watched her with renewed interest.

"Try them," she snorted to the cub.

"I'm not so sure," Dumpster warned her. "You want to poison him again?"

"He's got to eat," Casseomae said. "You said yourself it was probably the cherry seeds that sickened him."

"Yeah, *probably* is the important part of that proclamation."

But Casseomae ignored his concern and managed to get the child to eat some of the bulbs after he washed off the mud. Their foraging was interrupted by a howl, followed by others. Casseomae rose on her hind legs, dancing back and forth to catch their scent.

"How far away are they?" Dumpster asked.

"I can't tell." She dropped back to all fours and the child scuttled up beside her, blinking nervously up and down the river's edge.

"We've got to get out of Maul's territory," Pang said. "I think we should cross the river."

"And only head into another pack's territory," Dumpster said.

"At least now that his coat is gone, he has hardly a scent to attract attention."

"But he doesn't have the screen protecting him," the rat reminded him.

Casseomae faced Pang urgently. "Can we still reach the city if we cross?"

"Yes," Pang said. He splashed into the river, paddling into the currents.

With the cub on her back and Dumpster atop her head, Casseomae waded out to swim after the dog. The cub inhaled sharply as the cool water surrounded him. Casseomae's paws occasionally slapped against objects under the water, too smooth and flat to be rocks, and she guessed they were sunken debris from the Skinless Ones.

A howl reverberated off the water, and Casseomae paddled faster after Pang.

"Do you see them?" she asked.

"Not yet," Dumpster said, clinging to her ears. "But don't let that slow you down."

Pang reached the other bank first, and when Casseomae was able to touch, the child let go of her and splashed up on shore with evident relief.

"Quick," Casseomae said, butting him forward into the thick of the underbrush. Once they were in the shadows of the Forest, Casseomae went as close to the edge of the underbrush as she dared.

After a moment, a pair of wolves trotted down along the far shore, sniffing the ground. Then another wolf appeared and then several more. The breeze blowing off the river kept their scent from reaching her nose, and Casseomae had to hope their scent wasn't strong enough to reach the other side of the river. The wolves searched up and down the bank.

"They can't find where we went," Dumpster said with a happy squeak.

"See that wolf in the back?" Pang said. "That's Maul. I recognize him. And . . . what's Gnash doing here?"

Casseomae spied the pair of massive wolves coming

169

out from the trees. Gnash carried something in his mouth. "What's that? He's got the cub's coat!"

"Scratch it all!" Dumpster said. "Idiot cur! Why did you leave it for them to find?"

"They don't know what they've found," Casseomae said. "They'll never know that it belonged to—" Her words fell short as a large wolf came out from the shadows of the Forest. His coat was entirely black.

"Who is that?" Pang asked. "Have you seen that wolf before?"

As the enormous black wolf surveyed the river, more and more wolves came out along the banks. An army of wolves.

"Yes," Casseomae said. "I've seen him before. That's the Ogeema."

CHAPTER TWENTY-FIVE

They tore through the Forest, moving as far as they could from the river. Fear brewed in Casseomae's belly.

"That explains the fighting we heard last night," Pang panted beside her. "The Ogeema is even gathering packs that don't pay tribute to him!"

"I've never heard of packs banding together," Casseomae said incredulously.

Dumpster dug his claws into her head. "You still don't understand, do you, Cass? That cub of yours, that Old Devil, he's changed everything. By coming back, he's upset the order of the Forest. He's bringing about what's never been imagined before."

Casseomae felt the cub clinging tightly to her neck. "He's not doing anything."

"But he is," Pang said. "Just by being here. If the Companions are returning—"

"They're not returning," Casseomae said. "We saw them! They were all dead."

"There could be others," the dog said. "You don't know that there aren't. They just might not have come yet."

"And for the wolves," Dumpster said, "they're fighting to hold on to their rule over the Forest. I for one don't think the Skinless are coming back, but it doesn't really matter what I believe. The Ogeema has personally accompanied his wolves to hunt this cub down. He'll gather even more packs. We don't stand a chance of escaping now!"

Pang said, "They'll figure out we crossed the river."

"Then we've got to keep running," Casseomae growled.

"We can't outrun them," Dumpster said.

Pang panted anxiously. "If I remember right, there's a marsh nearby. It's not the quickest route and who knows what's out there. But the water will mask our trail."

Dumpster flicked his tail against Casseomae's ears. "As my old da used to say, '*Stay in the puddles and the voras it muddles.*'"

With heavy gray clouds hanging overhead, they soon reached the edge of the marsh. Splashing down into leaf-filled water and winding among the knobby roots and dense swatches of grass, they hurried as best they could as distant barks echoed through the Forest.

"Have they followed us?" the rat said later as he clung to the side of a cypress. Night was falling, and the howls had grown more faint but had not disappeared as they had hoped.

"Maybe." Pang gave him a slight grin. "We just have to hope they've been 'muddled.'"

Dumpster slipped from the cypress and splashed into the water. "I'm starting to think we were muddled to come this way," he said, climbing back to dry land.

The cub slept uneasily beside Casseomae that night. He was woken constantly by clouds of mosquitoes descending on him, and his skin was covered in red welts by the morning. The child scratched angrily as they followed the muddy high grounds crisscrossing the marsh. When the reeds grew too thick, they slogged through pools of stagnant water, filled with ancient debris and sheets of black plastic that Dumpster called garbage bags.

Later in the morning, the cub's frustrating battle with the mosquitoes got the better of him. Running down into a pool of dark water, he submerged himself except for his face.

"Poor cub," Casseomae said from the bank.

"We can't linger, Cass," Pang said. "We haven't

heard the wolves, but we need to keep the cub moving." He surveyed the sun. "This way."

Casseomae splashed down into the pool to nudge the cub out. He growled and rose, dripping with muck. After a few paces the cub stopped to scoop mud and rub it over his skin. He grinned with relief at Casseomae before trotting after Pang.

Deeper in the marsh, they came upon a mountainous relic tilted in the shallow water. Dumpster said it was a tanker, an ancient boat used by the Old Devils to cross the Wide Waters. But why or how it had come into this marsh, he had no guess.

The child kept his skin coated in mud, washing it off and adding more as it dried out in the sun's heat. His spirits were higher without the swarms of mosquitoes constantly covering him. He played with garbage he found, throwing broken chunks of glass at nesting ducks to make them take flight or scooping up tadpoles with smaller plastic bags.

The dog often loped ahead to investigate which way they should go. He would set their course in the morning by the rising sun and had a much better sense than Casseomae and Dumpster of which way they should travel through the marsh.

"We've not seen a Skinless den out here," Casseomae said. "Why are there so many of their things floating in these waters?"

"Oh, they were a rich tribe," Dumpster said. "They had so much, they would store what they couldn't keep in their dens out in places like these or even bury it in huge mounds beneath the earth. There are many fine tales of how Lord Murk raided these treasure hoards—"

Snarls erupted, and Casseomae looked up in time to see a blur of fur rush out from the grass. Pang, caught by surprise, was knocked over by the furious creature. He leaped to his feet, and the two tangled and snapped and yipped.

With a quick bite and a twist, Pang freed himself and stood facing another dog. "Hold off! I mean you no harm," he barked. "We didn't know this was your territory."

The dog was smaller than Pang, a hound of some sort with long dangling ears and protruding ribs. Her coat was speckled gray and black, and heavy teats hung from her underside.

"Why are you traveling with a bear?" she snarled.

Pang sniffed her. "You have a litter nearby, sister? She won't hurt your pups."

The hound eyed Casseomae and then she cocked her head as she caught sight of the child hiding behind Casseomae. "What is that? What strange creature travels with you?"

"Come see, sister," Pang said, grinning. "You won't believe what we've found."

The hound took a step forward, and Casseomae growled. "You don't know this cur," she said to Pang. "How do we know we can trust her?"

"She's a Faithful," Pang said. Then, looking back at the hound, he asked, "You are, aren't you?"

"Of course I am," she replied. "Why else would I be hiding out in this marsh? Think I want my pups killed by wolves?"

Pang circled around to the child and beat his tail against his leg, urging the child to follow him. "See. We have been rewarded, sister. Look what has returned!"

The hound flinched, lowering her head deferentially. Then she edged closer to the child, who was petting Pang's head. She sniffed. "No. Is that . . . can that be a Companion?"

"It is," Pang said, running up to lick the hound's nose and then leaping back to the child. "This is a Companion pup! The bear found him in the Forest."

"Bless my sniffer," the hound said, grinning up at the child and nearing so he could pet her speckled coat. "I never thought I would see one. Do you know what this means?"

"Of course! Of course!" Pang barked.

Dumpster slipped out from the grass and muttered, "Scratch me bald. Another cur?"

The hound stiffened when she saw him, but Pang

quickly snapped at her. "The rat is with us. Don't eat him."

"That's a warning, not a request," Dumpster said from behind Casseomae's front paw, "if you know what's good for you."

The hound looked back up, mesmerized by the child. "Come with me. We must get back to my pups. I want them to see the Companion."

They followed her to a metal container hidden in the weeds. Whimpers and whines greeted the hound as she returned. She slumped down inside as her litter of pups scrambled onto her stomach to nurse. Casseomae felt they couldn't be more than a week old. The child got down on his knees to crawl toward the pups, and Pang nipped at his shoulder.

"No, he's fine," the hound said. "Let him touch my pups. Let the Companion bless my children." She watched with pleasure as the child gently stroked the cooing, suckling pups.

Casseomae asked, "Do you have a pack?"

"Sometimes," she said. "There are others I've traveled with. But it's too dangerous these days to keep pups with a pack. I discovered this marsh when I had my first litter. Wolves and coyotes rarely hunt here. Tell me, where are the other Companions? Has the war begun?"

"The war?" Dumpster squeaked.

The hound glanced at Pang, who slunk a little lower. "Have you not told them?"

"Told us what?" Dumpster squeaked. "Oh, I knew we couldn't trust that scratchin' cur, Cass! Told you the day we first sniffed his traitorous hide."

"I'm no traitor," Pang yapped.

The pups whimpered, and the child hissed at Pang, batting him on the nose. The hound soothed her pups with licks as she coaxed them back to nursing.

"Then what's she talking about?" Casseomae asked. "What's this about a war?"

Pang eyed her apprehensively. "It's what we've been promised. For being Faithful."

The hound said, "They say the day will come when the Companions will return and wage a war against the wolves to reclaim the Forest."

Casseomae said, "And this will be your reward?"

"To live again safely in the dens of our Companions," the hound said. "No longer having to hide in swamps to deliver our young. No longer being hunted and killed by the wolves."

"But," Casseomae said slowly, "what will become of the Forest?"

The hound and Pang exchanged a glance.

A sickening feeling came over Casseomae. She had heard all her life of what it was like before the Turning, how the Forest had once been cut down, how the

Skinless Ones had driven the voras nearly into extinction. She looked at Dumpster. "What will become of my clan?"

The rat flicked his tail. "You know as well as I do, Cass."

Confusion and anger rose in Casseomae. She backed away from the den and paced out into the marsh. When she was away from the others, she swiped her claws against the ground and looked around at the desolate expanse of water and reeds. Garbage and rusting relics were everywhere. There was hardly a place in the Forest without the ruins of the Skinless Ones.

She thought of the Ogeema and his army of wolves. Was he searching for her cub in order to protect his authority? She had always despised the Ogeema as a ruler full of cruelty and vanity. But what if he was motivated by something else, something she had not considered until now? What if he was trying to protect the Forest?

She suddenly thought of what the cub had done to the buck. His thunderous weapon had been brutal, more devastating than any claw or tooth that the voras of the Forest possessed.

As she slumped to the ground, the child came out from the hound's den. He gave her a questioning whine, then slowly crept over and put his hands on her snout. She licked him, scraping the mud from his arms.

"Are you letting those stupid curs upset you?"

Dumpster emerged from the grass, wagging his whiskers at her. "You don't really believe their nonsense?"

"What do you mean?" Casseomae said.

"That the Companions will take the Forest back from the wolves."

She lifted her head as he circled around to a new spot, where he sniffed up at the child. "He's only one Old Devil," Dumpster said, "and he's hardly that anymore. He's your cub. You're teaching him how to live with the Forest. You've protected him as well as that hound has protected her litter. Don't listen to them, Cass. There won't be any war. There are no other Companions. He's your cub, and you'll raise him to be a mushroom-headed bear just like you."

She snorted. The child laughed as the air from her nose blew back his hair. She nudged him with her snout. With a chirp, he dug his fingers into her fur, squeezing her as tightly as he could.

"You're right," she said to Dumpster. "But first we have to find the island."

CHAPTER TWENTY-SIX

"I wish you could come with us, sister," Pang said to the hound the following morning.

"Me too," she said. "But I will tell the packs the good news when I see them again. I will tell them to be ready."

Dumpster lashed his tail irritably, but Casseomae gave him a grunt to stay quiet.

As they set off, the hound followed them a few steps, her eyes locked on the child. "My pups will grow up in a better world," she barked. "The end of the wolves' reign is near. Travel upwind. Travel safely."

Once they were out of earshot of the hound, Dumpster said, "Are you really so superstitious as to believe all that nonsense, cur?"

"Is it wrong to have hope?" Pang said, leading the

way through the maze of high ground that crisscrossed the marsh.

"Hope is one thing," Dumpster said. "Survival is another."

"Hope is how our kind has survived," the dog said. "It's how we all survive. Your mischief set off in search of a land without voras. You scoffed at them. And now we've heard from the Auspectres that the Havenlands exist. Your mischief might be living free in those happy lands right now."

"I'll believe in the Havenlands when we see them," the rat said. "Until then I'll just *hope* I don't wind up in the bottom of the Ogeema's belly."

As they foraged midday by a deeper creek, Pang wandered off to investigate the terrain ahead. "The Forest is nearby," he told them when he returned, "but there's no way to know if the local pack has joined the Ogeema. I think we should stay in the marsh. It's slow going, but it's safer."

They all agreed. The marsh ahead had less high ground and they were forced to wade through reedy water that made Casseomae nervous. It would be hard to defend themselves or escape if they were attacked, but fortunately they smelled nothing more than otters as they traveled. By nightfall, they were glad to find a highway that cut through the marsh. Exhausted from all the slogging, they sank to the broken concrete and slept.

At dawn, Pang said, "The sun rises from down this highway trail. It won't be entirely out of the water, but I think we'll have an easier time this way."

"Do you know how much farther we have to go to reach the city?" Casseomae asked.

"Another sleep or two, I suspect," Pang said. "We're nearly out of the marsh."

But as the sun reached its highest point that afternoon, enormous towers could be seen in the distance.

"Look," Dumpster squeaked. "Skyscrapers!"

"Is that the city?" Casseomae asked.

"Pluck my whiskers if it isn't," the rat replied.

The skyscrapers looked to Casseomae like the broken trunks of trees, thick and dark, ascending straight up and snapped at the tops as if by a windstorm. The highway soon joined others at the end of the marsh. Without the Forest to bury the trails beneath vegetation, Casseomae could see how numerous the Skinless Ones' paths could be. She would never have known which one to take had it not been for Pang, and even he seemed to select the best one based purely on guesswork and by aiming their noses for the growing skyscrapers.

Although they got closer by sunset, the city was still far off. Pang stopped them at an overpass. "Like I told you before, strange tribes live around this city. It will be dark soon, and I don't like the idea of being too close when we sleep."

"We should stay here for the night, then?" Casseomae asked.

"It would be best," the dog said.

Pang trotted off in search of puddles and the child followed him, climbing on cars and poking branches through their shattered windows. Casseomae loped after them and paused at the crest of the overpass. She could see the city better now, rising from the far side of a river. Trees grew thickly like underbrush beneath the towering skyscrapers. The highway ahead cut through a swath of smaller buildings, broken and collapsed ruins of concrete and glass.

Dumpster was eating a beetle nearby when Casseomae heard him say, "Where's the pup?"

She swung around and nearly hit Pang as he passed by. The dog circled and looked back the way he'd come. "He's playing down there."

A toppled car was in her way, and as she came around it, she saw the cub at the bottom of the concrete trail, squatting in front of a large vehicle, chirping to himself.

"You left him alone?" Casseomae woofed.

"He's just down there," Pang said. "He's fine. He's—"

From around the vehicle, Rend and her rout emerged and surrounded the child.

CHAPTER TWENTY-SEVEN

Casseomae unleashed a full-throated roar as she charged down the trail.

Rend signaled with a glance, and two of the coyotes descended on the child, one grabbing his ankle, the other locking his jaws onto his wrist. The child screamed in pain. They pulled him off his feet and began tugging him toward the tree line. The cub fought, kicking his feet and swinging his fists.

Casseomae barreled toward them, strings of saliva slinging from her teeth. "Let go of him!"

"Stop where you are," Rend called, "or I'll have them go for his throat."

Casseomae bounced angrily on locked front legs. Rend yipped at her rout, and the two coyotes let go of the cub, forming a tight circle around him with the others.

Pang stepped in front of Casseomae. "Wait, Cass, we can do this smart."

"Yes, you can," Rend said. She kept her head low and her ears back, calm and cold. "First, do you understand what hunts you?"

Casseomae's breathing came in heavy, furious snorts.

Rend went on. "The Ogeema has packs searching all over the Forest. He himself is not far behind you, leading a charge of wolves of a size not seen since Taka-Dirge's army. All for your . . . abhorrent cub."

The slender coyote paced back and forth, her bushy tail making deliberate swipes. "I have borne many litters, Casseomae. I know what it means to protect a pup. When your den is found by a wolf pack and you are forced to choose between losing your pups and losing your own life . . . well, I know what it's like to be in that position also. It's a painful choice but hardly a choice at all if you think about it. It's simply the way of the Forest."

She looked back at the cub with her yellow eyes. "He doesn't belong here, bear," she said. "This is no longer his world. He'll never survive, and I'm afraid there's nowhere—"

"There is," Casseomae growled. "There is, and I'm taking him there. And you and those wolves will never find him."

Rend turned up her snout and gave several high yips.

"You sound like you've been talking to the Auspectres," she laughed. "Have they sent you to this city? Let me caution you against heeding those vulture witches too closely. They crave a meal. Nothing would please them more than to have a fine, fat bear carcass, not to mention a tasty Skinless One and his cur Companion."

Pang snarled. "Don't listen to her lies."

"The Auspectres are more likely than not sending you to your slaughter for their own feasting pleasure," Rend said.

Casseomae could not help but think how the Auspectres had told her she would have to walk over the water to reach the island where the cub would be safe. No bridge that large could remain. Were the Auspectres leading her to a trap?

She shook off the doubt. She knew she couldn't trust anything Rend told her.

The cub was no longer whimpering. He didn't look frightened. His skin streaked with mud and his hair tangled with burrs and leaves, he sat in the middle of the circling coyotes licking his bleeding wrist. His eyes were narrowed as he searched for something.

"You won't leave here with my cub," Casseomae growled.

"As I said before," Rend said, "there's hardly a choice at all. Attack us and we'll kill him. We can lead the Ogeema back here later to show him the carcass. Or you and the cur can let us take him alive. You may leave unharmed, knowing you did your best but that you had no other choice."

Casseomae popped her jaws angrily. The other four in Rend's rout flinched, watching her with unblinking yellow eyes. The child slid a hand slowly to one side.

Rend flattened her ears at Casseomae. "Stay where you are. Don't make a mis—"

The child lunged for a stick on the ground and snapped it in half beneath his foot. Before the coyotes could react, the child drove the sharp end of the stick into the hip of the nearest coyote, who yowled and twisted. With a swing, the child cracked the heavy end of the stick against another coyote's head.

Casseomae charged. Rend cast a quick glance at her and then retreated with the rest of her rout. The coyote with the bleeding leg barely made it back to the Forest before Pang caught up, barking and snapping at his tail. Pang circled back to where Casseomae was sniffing the cub's wounds and licking the blood from his ankle.

"Is he hurt?" Pang asked.

"They didn't bite him deep," she said, "but we can't stay here. She'll go straight to the Ogeema. We've got to get into that city tonight."

Dumpster had emerged from where he'd been hiding and sprang around in frantic circles. "You can't roam a city at night! It's not like the Forest. The smells aren't the same, and the terrain's all different. You'll never know a hunter is tracking you until his teeth clamp into your neck."

"What else are we supposed to do?" Casseomae asked.

Pang was staring at the city, the last of the sun's setting rays illuminating the top of a particularly tall skyscraper. "We just have to reach that den there. And then we'll know where the Havenlands are. Then we'll know where to go."

CHAPTER TWENTY-EIGHT

They raced past the ruins of the Skinless Ones' buildings lining the highway. Casseomae was uncomfortable with their quick pace. Charging into unfamiliar terrain chafed against her instincts. The cub ran, not with the frightful jitteriness he once had and not with a carefree sense of play either. He had already learned a great deal on their journey. He growled and held his stick at the ready like a fighter, and she was proud of her cub for it.

But it made her no less nervous.

The highway regularly split off in a number of directions. Pang was having trouble finding which route was the best to follow.

"This can't be right," Dumpster squeaked as the night darkened around them.

The wide double path of the highway had disappeared, and they were now among ruined buildings on a narrow path cluttered with relics.

Pang sniffed side to side. "We've got to reach the river. The city lies on the other bank. From what I remember, the Companion paths that cross over the river are all collapsed."

"If there aren't bridges," Dumpster asked, "how are we supposed to get across? Swim?"

"No," he said. "Not with what lives in the water."

"Then what do we do?" Casseomae asked.

"There's a narrow metal passage," Pang said, "like one of the lick-trick city towers. It's fallen over the river. It's somewhere nearby. We can go over that, I think."

Dumpster clicked his teeth. "You *think* . . ."

A cry cut through the night, a strange trumpeting call. The child crouched, holding his stick out with shaking hands.

"What was that?" Casseomae said.

Pang whined. "I told you strange creatures inhabit this place."

"What sort of city is this?" Dumpster said. "There's nothing like that where I'm from."

Pang trotted ahead, sniffing around the corners of buildings as he led them forward. Soon they could see the dark waters of the river between the ruins. The concrete was covered with silt and mud from the river's floods. Weeds and trees grew thicker, and the sound of night birds and tree-dwelling creatures was louder.

Casseomae spied something watching them from a branch overhead. At first she thought it was a large squirrel with a long tail wrapped around its branch. But as they got closer, she realized it looked nothing like a squirrel. In fact it looked somewhat like the cub, like a strange version of a Skinless One except it had a coat of fur.

"What is that?" she growled.

As Pang and Dumpster looked up, the creature sprang with powerful back legs to a higher branch and vanished into rustling leaves in the treetop.

"I couldn't see it," Pang said.

"Doesn't matter," Dumpster said. "Keep going."

Pang led them past several more buildings until at last he barked, "There!"

Resting atop the roof of a building was one end of a metal tower. It was crumpled and rusted, but from what Casseomae could see the structure did extend across the river. "How do we get up there?" she asked.

"The stairs," Dumpster said.

"The what?" Pang asked.

"Stairs," he repeated. "Don't you know? In these taller Old Devil dens, they have stairs to help you climb to the top. You see short ones all the time outside houses. Just go inside. I'll show you."

They found the opening to the building. Lying before the entranceway was the remains of a strange deer. It had an exceptionally long neck and had to have been three times as tall as any deer Casseomae had ever seen before. But strangest of all was its hide. Although it was bloodied and rotting, she could make out spots all over its coat, large brown blots against a field of tawny yellow.

"I have no idea," Pang said, leaping over the carcass to get into the building.

Once they were all inside, Dumpster said, "Go down that hall . . . that passage. They should be somewhere around."

Sniffing at every surface, they walked around until Casseomae felt nauseous at being so enclosed. "I don't like this," she growled. "I feel trapped."

"It's got to be scratchin' somewhere around," Dumpster said. "Look!"

Through an opening in a wall, there were the leveled concrete steps she had indeed seen often outside Skinless's dens. But there were so many in here. As she followed the others up the stairs, she felt a certain dizziness climbing inside a building without the comfort of earth under her claws.

Along the way they saw other passages, but Dumpster said, "Keep climbing." At last they reached the end of the stairs, where they found a closed door. Dumpster rose on his hind legs. "You'll have to break this door, old bear. Push your weight against it."

Casseomae reared up on her back legs and leaned her forepaws against the door. It groaned but didn't break. She dropped down and moved back a step before butting her head heavily against the metal. "That hurt," she growled.

"Just hit it harder," the rat squeaked.

Before Casseomae did it again, the cub chirped something. Then he reached out to turn several things with his delicate fingers. The door swung open.

"Or we could do that," Dumpster said.

To Casseomae's relief they came out into the open air atop the building. It was not nearly as high as the skyscrapers that lay on the far side of the river, but from where they were, she could see where the tower reached the other bank.

"We cross this?" she asked Pang.

"Unless you have another idea," he said.

Casseomae reached up with her claws to pull herself atop the fallen tower. The metal creaked and a portion snapped, dropping the entire structure down a fraction. She growled uneasily and took a few steps along the top. Dumpster scampered up ahead of her.

Pang leaped but could not get a good hold on the surface with his claws. The child grabbed him around the waist and hoisted the dog up with a grunt. Pang whined and scrambled with his forepaws until Casseomae took his loose scruff in her teeth and pulled him up.

"Thanks," he said, finding his footing on the metal.

"Don't fall," she said.

"Easy for you to say, bear. Your kind is good at climbing."

"Not on relics like this," she grunted.

Once the child scrambled up, the four began easing across the tower. Pang flattened to his belly to crawl ever more slowly. The child was just behind him, also on all fours and breathing heavily through his teeth. Only Dumpster had no trouble and ran forward and back urging the others to hurry.

When they came out over the river, a trumpeting call stilled them. Dumpster shot to Casseomae and stared at her, nose to nose. "It's below us," he whispered with twittering whiskers.

Another cry broke, louder and nearer. Heavy steps sloshed through water. Whatever they were, they were huge. Casseomae leaned to one side to peer over the edge.

The wolves had always ruled over the bears not because of their size but because of their numbers and ferocity. Casseomae had always believed the bears to be the biggest creatures in the Forest. What she saw below dwarfed even Chief Alioth.

An immense shadow moved against the moonlit

waters. It flapped huge ears and lifted what appeared to be a snakelike tail, except it was coming from the creature's face. Protruding from its mouth were two long white fangs. Casseomae knew they could spear her through her gut if the beast was hunting her.

"Rat," she whispered. "Does your mischief's Memory have a name for that?"

"Not a spittin' utterance," he answered.

The creature blasted a stream of water from the protuberance and curled it around atop its head to give another of the trumpeting calls. Other creatures answered. As Casseomae looked around she saw a whole pack of the monsters filling the shallows of the river's edge.

"For Murk's sake, don't slip," Dumpster said. "Those things will tear you to pieces."

Pang whimpered pitifully and scooted against Casseomae's rear. "Go. Just go. Faster, please. Before one of those things snatches me away with its serpent nose!"

Casseomae went faster, walking steadily with one paw behind the other until they were over the far bank. The base of the tower, where it had broken, lay ahead. Casseomae knew getting off would prove difficult since the tower was wider on this end.

Dumpster went down first, leaping along the metal framework until he got to the bottom. Casseomae found it to be a bit like coming down the branches of a tree, but the metal was not so easy to hold on to. Halfway down, her claws slipped and she fell to the rough stone.

Grunting with embarrassment, she rose and shook her coat. "Come on down," she called.

The cub sat atop the tower beside Pang, looking anxiously from the dog to the ground. He reached his arm around Pang's waist, but Pang gave a snarl and squirmed from his grasp.

"He can't carry you down," Casseomae said.

"I know," Pang said, licking an apology to the cub's cheek. "He was just trying to help."

"Come," Casseomae snorted to the child.

The cub climbed down swiftly with his limber arms and legs. At the bottom, he chirped at Pang and waved his hands.

"You're going to have to jump," Dumpster said.

"I'll break my legs!"

"How else are you going to get down?" Casseomae said.

"I don't know." Pang paced around, looking for some escape.

"Can you go back and find another way across?" she asked.

"I told you, all the bridges are broken."

"You could swim," Dumpster said.

Pang yipped, "And get eaten by one of those creatures!"

"The creatures are on the far bank," Casseomae

called to Pang. "If you jump into the river near this bank, they may not come after you."

"You don't know that!" He tucked his tail miserably between his legs.

Casseomae grunted. "Well, you could wait there for us and hope—"

A wolf howl, long and piercing, cut through the night.

"They're coming!" Casseomae said.

Pang turned and scampered back along the tower until he was over the river. With a tiny yip, he leaped, disappearing into the dark with only a faint splash echoing a moment later.

CHAPTER TWENTY-NINE

The calls of the wolves grew louder. "We've got to go," Dumpster squeaked.

"We can't leave the dog," Casseomae said.

"Actually, we can," Dumpster said.

Casseomae grunted at the cub to follow her. They climbed down through the debris and vines to the river's edge. She smelled the leafy water and felt mud beneath her paws.

"Pang," she huffed. "Where are you?"

She saw a ripple of moonlight on the water and then the dog, paddling furiously toward the shore. When he climbed up, he didn't even take the time to shake the water from his fur but bolted through the weeds past them. When they found him, he was shaking with fright under an overturned car.

"They almost had me," he whimpered. "Almost jabbed me with those giant teeth."

"No, they didn't," Casseomae said. "They were all the way on the other side. I don't think they even smelled you."

Howls reverberated off the buildings lining the river. "At least the wolves don't have a Companion to boost them up onto the tower," Pang said. "They won't be able to cross."

"They'll figure out another way," Dumpster said. "That many wolves won't fear swimming, even with those monsters about. We've got to find shelter before they pick up our scent."

"Where do we go?" Casseomae said.

"Scratch me bald if I know," Dumpster replied.

Pang eased out from under the car and shook the water from his fur. Still trembling, he sniffed around. The city was a dense place. It felt to Casseomae as if she were a tiny cub in the most enormous thicket. Debris and relics were everywhere. Trees broke through the cracks of concrete, but they were dwarfed by the buildings, which nearly blocked out the ruddy glow of dawn in the sky above. Noises groaned all around. Not the noises of animals, but sounds Casseomae could only attribute to restless metal and concrete.

Up close, the skyscrapers were more encased in ivy and vegetation than what she had seen from a distance.

They were pocked with holes. Shrubs and trees grew from them, even up high. A flock of birds took flight from a shattered window, circling the building in a cloud before roosting again on a neighboring skyscraper.

"I don't know if I can lead you well in here," Pang said.

Casseomae felt it was more than unfamiliar terrain that was hindering the dog. The leap into the river and the fear of the pursuing pack compounded by the dread of what monstrous voras might stalk this city had nearly paralyzed the poor dog with fright. The child knelt, stroking his wet fur and trying to comfort him.

"You know these cities," Casseomae said to Dumpster. "This might not be yours, but you have to show us where to go."

The rat flicked his tail and rose up on his hind legs. "Oh, all right," he said. He scampered ahead, dancing over the broken glass and around the drifts of leaves and sticks. "We have to find a skyscraper tall enough to see the Wide Waters."

Casseomae lumbered after him with Pang on one side and the cub on the other. Many of the paths were blocked by enormous sections of tumbled skyscrapers. Dumpster had to backtrack several times, and they had hardly gotten far before they heard trumpeting cries from the river and the snarls of wolves.

"We need to move faster," Casseomae growled. "They're crossing the river."

"Into that alley," Dumpster ordered.

"The what?" Pang whined.

Dumpster didn't answer. He simply set off through a gap between two of the buildings. Debris and saplings cluttered the passageway. It was a tight squeeze for Casseomae, but she managed. There was the smell of foxes and skunks as well as the scent of creatures she did not recognize. Emerging on the other side, they reached a more open area.

"That one," Dumpster said, pointing with his nose. "Don't you think?"

Casseomae surveyed the buildings. Many were sheared off partway up, but one seemed mostly intact. Its exterior was not pocked with the holes of broken glass and weeds that covered the others.

"Good enough," Casseomae said.

They wound their way through the debris until they found the base of the building. "How do we get in?" Pang said, surveying the stone front.

"Follow me," Dumpster said. "There should be a doorway on one of the other sides."

Coming around the corner, they smelled the sharp tang of a rotting carcass. The carcass itself was too mauled for any of them to identify, but Casseomae thought it had the familiar scent of bear.

Nothing in the Forest hunted bears. What could have done this? She sniffed to see if its hunter was lurking nearby but didn't smell anything alive.

Dumpster headed through the entranceway, a wide opening of broken glass and rusting metal. The interior was fashioned from smooth wood, although it was mostly choked in ivy and creeper.

"Stairs," Dumpster said, heading toward a wide expanse of half-rotten wooden stairs leading up into the darkness. Water dripped down from somewhere above, the *plip plop*s echoing around the room. The rat stopped. "The problem is that when the wolves find us, they'll be able to follow our scent easy as itchin'. We need a way to block the path."

"Let's worry about that after we're safely inside," Pang said, starting up the steps. Dumpster dashed after him, with Casseomae and the cub following right behind. They had only gotten halfway up when Casseomae heard groans beneath her paws. Before she could turn back, the stairs collapsed.

The cub fell with her, shrieking as he grabbed her fur. Casseomae hit the ground hard and lay half-dazed. Dust plumed up around them from the ruined staircase.

The cub stood and pulled at Casseomae's foreleg, whimpering.

"I'm not hurt," she said, standing to shake off the dirt.

Pang and Dumpster peered down at them from the ledge above. "That's not exactly what I meant by blocking the path, you heavy oaf," the rat squeaked.

"Can the pup climb up here?" Pang barked down.

Casseomae grunted and looked up at the dangling remains of the staircase. "It's too far."

"Well, there should be other ways up," Dumpster said. "There're often a few sets of stairs in these sky-scrapers. Go look around, and we'll wait for you."

Casseomae quickly found other passages, but she didn't get very far before she was blocked by debris and waterlogged, collapsed ceilings. The cub tried more of the doors, but none would budge. Casseomae butted against them with her full weight. The only one that broke open led back outside.

They were standing in the narrow alley between the skyscraper and its neighboring building. In one direc-tion the alley was blocked by one of the large metal con-tainers that were Dumpster's namesake. The other way led back out to the open area in front of the building. She had started in that direction when a wolf's shadow crossed the alley's entrance.

She froze, but the wolf hadn't seen them. A series of yips and barks announced that the wolves had found their scent at the front of the building.

The child whimpered, pressing close to her. She gave him a quick reassuring nudge with her nose and snorted, "Stay calm, cub. I'm here."

More of the wolves passed outside the alley. Casseomae slowly backed up. At any moment one of them would smell her and lead the rest down to where she was cornered.

She would fight them. She would have no choice. But she could not defend the cub against them all.

The cub was no longer pressed against her. He was standing at the dumpster, leaping for something above. It was a metal framework, like a smaller version of one of the electricity towers, except it was attached to the side of the building. The cub was trying to grab the lowest section, but it was just out of his reach.

A growl resounded down the alley.

Casseomae turned to see a wolf at the entrance. His hackles were raised and even in the dim light his teeth shone. "Ogeema!" he barked. "I have them."

Casseomae whipped around. "You have to get up," she grunted. She pushed her nose under the cub's hips and hoisted him up. The cub caught hold of the metal structure. He grunted and pulled until he pitched a leg over the frame and began to climb.

Casseomae turned to confront the wolf. He was joined by others, until the entranceway was darkened by their numbers.

"Let me through," a whispered voice commanded.

The wolves stepped aside for the massive form of the Ogeema. Casseomae pounded a forepaw to the ground. The Ogeema would not take her easily.

"You stupid, traitorous bear," the Ogeema said. "You bring shame to your clan."

Casseomae looked up. The cub was standing on the lowest platform, panting for breath. He leaned over the edge and called down to her.

She had gotten him this far. She had to hope Pang could lead the cub to safety from here. But how? Even if the wolves could not climb the stairs, the cub and Pang and Dumpster would not be able to get past them. They would be trapped.

Anger surged through Casseomae's body. Saliva dripped from her teeth as she roared defiance at the Ogeema.

The cub shook the metal framework, crying out for her.

"Go, cub!" she said, not wanting him to see what the wolves would do to her. "Get to the others!"

"Others?" the Ogeema asked coolly. "I have smelled the cur who travels with you. But what is the other? Some sort of vole?"

"Vole? I'm not a vole," Dumpster squealed. He and Pang were peering through a broken window next to the cub. "I'm a rat, you stupid underlicker."

The Ogeema snarled up at him. "Most likely you'll taste no better than a vole." He lowered his head and paced down the alley toward Casseomae.

The child rattled the metal, shaking it furiously.

"Pang," Casseomae called. "Get the cub—" But before she finished, the metal frame that the cub had climbed dropped suddenly. Casseomae ducked as it stopped just above her ears with a clank.

Dumpster shrieked, "Climb, you idiot bear. You can climb that ladder!"

Casseomae hooked her claws on the metal, pulling with all her might as the Ogeema and the pack rushed toward her. With jaws snapping at her haunches, she tugged herself up the groaning metal, the entire structure coming loose under her weight.

The cub disappeared through the window after Pang and Dumpster. Casseomae had just dug her forepaws into the rotten edge of the window when the metal tower broke free, landing on the Ogeema and several of the other wolves, who yelped in pain.

Casseomae hung from the window, then with a kick of her back paws slid through.

Two of the wolves lay motionless under the broken tangle of metal. But the Ogeema stood free of the structure. With blood dripping down his nose, he stared up at Casseomae.

"We will be waiting," he whispered. "We will be waiting right down here."

CHAPTER THIRTY

The child clung tightly to Casseomae, not wanting to let go. She grunted kindly to him, "I'm all right. Thanks to you and that falling metal thing."

"The Old Devils called those fire escapes," Dumpster said. "They would climb them if there was a brush fire. That way they could get above the flames and back into the safety of their dens."

Pang gave a low whine and looked up at the water-stained ceiling. Despite having only one window, the shadowy den was full of leaves and piles of blown-in debris. Mushrooms grew on an ancient moldy piece of furniture in the corner. A pair of panicked sparrows flapped around in the uppermost corners of the room before finding their way out the window.

Casseomae felt the anger and fear that had propelled

her through the night starting to fade. They might have been trapped, but they were safe, at least for the moment. Hunger reclaimed her instincts, and she set off through the building to see if there was anything to eat. Her cub followed her. Pang and Dumpster, their eyes brimming with exhaustion, lay down where they were.

She was used to nosing around in old Skinless dens, but this one felt particularly cramped. As she crawled over piles of debris and wound in and out of mildew-speckled rooms, she heard the sounds of birds. Coming through a doorway into a room filled with morning light, she saw shrubs, vines, and saplings growing thickly where the tall windows had shattered.

Songbirds and starlings gathered by the dozens to feast on berries growing on the shrubs. Casseomae lunged at a goldfinch, but the bird was too fast. Along with the others, it zipped through the window and flew off.

Casseomae began eating the berries. The cub plucked one and sniffed it before nibbling. He seemed to feel that the berries were acceptable and ate several before kneeling down to sip rainwater that had gathered in a broken white relic. Casseomae flopped lazily to the floor, chewing on a cluster of berries and watching the cub.

At some point she slipped into sleep. When she woke the sun was higher but still behind the towering skyscrapers surrounding their building. Her cub was gone and she got up quickly, sniffing after him.

She found him in the next room, a smaller den with only one unbroken window. There were not so many leaves in here. The child sat with his legs crossed, chirping in the softest whisper. Casseomae saw that he was holding something. It was some sort of device, but not a luminous screen like he had carried before. It smelled of plastic, and as her eyes adjusted to the dimness, she saw the thing looked like a small version of the cub—pink and furless but for a long tuft of sparkly yellow hair sprouting from the top of its head.

The cub happily moved one of its arms up and down. Then he squeezed the thing to his chest before holding it out to continue talking to it.

Casseomae snorted, startling the cub. He stood and tucked the thing behind his back. He grunted at Casseomae, a noise that sounded vaguely to her like he was asking something.

"Leave that alone," Casseomae said.

The cub held it protectively against his chest.

"No," she said. "Leave it here. It stinks."

The cub whimpered but placed the little pink thing on the floor. He spent a moment moving its arms and legs, arranging it, before he came over to nuzzle Casseomae's neck.

"Are you hungry—" she began to ask, but a violent burst of barking from Pang erupted a few rooms away. Casseomae hurried through the doorway, huffing as she ran to the first room, where she found Pang barking at a hole in the wall.

"What is it?" Casseomae asked. "What's in there?"

"I don't know," the dog said. "I was asleep when I heard his squeak."

"Whose squeak?" she asked.

"The rat," Pang answered. "Dumpster. Something got him."

CHAPTER THIRTY-ONE

Casseomae sniffed at the hole. It was too small for her to get more than her nose in, too small even for Pang to get his head through. The inside was a shallow tunnel of wood running up behind the wall. She smelled the rat's panic scent and something else, too: a small vora.

A shrill squeak came from in the wall, followed by a scuffle and the scratching of claws.

"It's climbing up with him," Casseomae said.

She rose on her hind legs and brought her forepaws down against the wall. With a few blows, she opened a hole. She tore out chunks of white powdery material with her claws, but the rat and its attacker had already gone higher.

"It's no good," Pang said. "It's carried him up."

The child seemed to know what to do. He barked at them and ran from the room. Casseomae and Pang followed.

The cub found a nearby set of stairs and started climbing. Pang hurried past Casseomae as she sniffed at the stairs. They were metal, not wood, so she hoped they wouldn't be rotten. But metal could rust and fall apart too.

With tentative steps, Casseomae ascended to find the cub and Pang in a room full of weeds and broken glass. The dog barked fiercely at a section of moss-covered wall where the child was kicking open a hole.

Something growled inside, shuffling and scratching to get away. The cub kicked again, and suddenly a cat, a slim tabby, leaped out of the wall and sprang across the room toward the door. The cat had Dumpster in its teeth.

Pang, Casseomae, and the cub hurried after the cat as it vaulted up the steps. There were other cats on the stairs, who howled and hissed at the intruders as they chased the cat off the stairs and into a darkened room.

The cat slunk back, his teeth locked on Dumpster's neck. Other cats—sleek black ones, fluffy ones of filthy white, calicos and grays and tabbies—poured into the room after them, slinking against the walls and hiding around the rotten furniture. Dumpster cursed venom-ously and wriggled to get free of the tabby's jaws.

Pang barked, "Let him go, you vile puss, before I tear you to pieces!"

The dog darted forward, and the tabby dropped Dumpster. The rat staggered free as Pang stood over him, bringing his vicious jaws around to warn off the other cats.

Dumpster staggered back against Pang's leg, blood on the fur at the top of his neck.

"I want him, dears," a black-and-white cat hissed.

"No, he's mine," the tabby called out. "I found him first."

"You lost him, coward fangs," another spat from atop a ledge of wood. "He belongs to us all now."

"Yours!" Dumpster said in disbelief. "I don't belong to any of you."

"But you do, my dear," a gray growled. "You are our gift. From the queen. Mother Death brought you for us."

Glowing eyes surrounded them, hungry deep-throated growls filling the room.

"You clowder of underlickers are crazy," Dumpster said. "Get back, before my friends—"

"The queen will have your friends," a long-haired white said. "They belong to her. But you, my little dear . . . you are ours."

"Nobody is eating anybody," Casseomae said, "so you cats might as well clear out."

"That is not how her queendom works," a cat said.

"She provides us with prey. Viand birds. Crawly viands. Creeping viands. Micey viands."

"I'm not a mouse, you hairball!" Dumpster said.

"But you are a present," the tabby said. "I didn't get any of the others of your kind. You should have been mine."

Dumpster looked as if his eyes might burst. "Others of my kind?"

"We thought we'd eaten all the Vorago speakers," one of the cats said. "Then more arrived not a few suns ago."

"My mischief!" the rat said. "What did you do to them?"

"We ate as many as we could catch before she decided her gift had been too generous."

Dumpster looked faint again. He staggered a step, mumbling, "My . . . my mischief . . . no."

"Which of you is the queen?" Pang barked. "Who rules here?"

The cats drew back against the walls, hiding under furniture and debris. "Mother Death is not here," one said. "You would already be hers, cur, if she was."

Casseomae huffed. "No puss hunts a dog."

"She will have you too, old bear," the tabby answered with a malicious glint in his eyes. "Mother Death has eaten bigger bears than you."

"And she is fond of the apes as well," a cat added,

looking at the cub. "Even a strange hairless one like your friend there. She will be glad to know there are more about the city."

An ape? Casseomae had no idea what sort of creature that was. Dumpster was right; there was something mad about this clowder.

The child knelt down to inspect Dumpster, touching the wounds on his back.

"I'm fine," the rat said, leaping onto the cub's arm and scuttling up onto his shoulder.

"We're leaving," Casseomae said, moving to the door. Pang and the child followed behind her. "Tell your queen she'll have to find another present."

The mob watched them go, tails lashing. "You can tell her yourself, old bear," one of the cats called, "when you meet her."

At the staircase, Pang said, "I'm really not liking this."

Casseomae started up the stairs. "Let's go look for those towers the Auspectres told us about."

The climb was long, but after seemingly endless sets of steps, the stairs ended at a door. The cub worked something on the door's face and then opened it with a faint squeak of rust. They came out into bright sunlight on the top of the skyscraper. The city with its towers of vine-coated concrete spread out below them.

Pang slunk flat to the ground. "Don't go too close to

the edge," he whined. "You'll tip the building over and we'll fall."

"If this thing hasn't collapsed yet," Dumpster said from the cub's shoulder, "it probably won't today."

Pang lay whimpering as Casseomae and the cub walked slowly to the edge of the roof. When they got there, the child gasped and backed away. But the height did not bother Casseomae. She poked her nose over the edge and peered down, thinking it must be like what a bird sees. The trees and buildings below were tiny. She could just make out the wolves waiting for them. How would she ever fight her way through them all? She snorted. They would simply have to find the best time, possibly when the wolves were sleeping or out hunting.

Grasping the cub's hair with his forelegs to steady himself, Dumpster stood on his hind legs and peered into the distance. "What's out there?" he said.

Casseomae knew her eyesight was not as good as a vulture's, but it was better than Dumpster's at seeing distances. In the direction where the sun rose, the city gave way to the Forest, a rolling haze of green oaks and poplars and hickories. The river that bordered the city cut through the woods, winding toward the horizon, where a silver flatness shimmered. The Wide Waters, she realized. And just before that silver shimmer, at the most distant edge of the Forest, strange forms rose above the treetops.

"I see towers," she said.

Pang stood tentatively. "They don't look like lick-trick city towers."

"What do they look like?" Dumpster asked.

Casseomae narrowed her small eyes. The dog was right. They were not like the skeletal framework of the Auspectres' towers or the fallen tower they had used to cross over the river. They rose smooth and gray like the trunk of a lightning-struck pine. There were three of them. At the tops, flat fins revolved in lazy circles.

"It looks like they have wings," she said.

"Wings?" the rat squeaked. "The spinning trees!"

"Just as the Auspectres said," Pang added, coming up beside them. "And look there, Cass. Can you see in the middle? It looks like each has a red glowing eye."

Dumpster lashed his tail. "Glowing?"

"Yes, I think he's right," Casseomae said. "Each has a light."

"Lights!" Dumpster clawed around on the child's shoulder, and the cub picked him off, holding him gently in his hand. "But how can that be?"

Behind them they heard a trembling growl, like the cats' but much deeper. Casseomae turned, her nose filling with a strange new scent. In the darkness of the doorway, a pair of large golden eyes watched them. A head emerged from the shadows. It was a cat, but far larger than any puss, larger even than the cougar.

It padded slowly onto the roof, a massive orange cat with black stripes like scars raked across its body. Casseomae had no doubt that it was at least twice the weight of the largest bear in her sloth. But what cat grew this large?

Pang snarled as the cub huddled behind Casseomae.

"Those pusses," Dumpster said. "They really weren't crazy. That's their queen, isn't it?"

Mother Death rumbled.

CHAPTER THIRTY-TWO

Casseomae drew her claws across the concrete roof, popping her jaws threateningly.

Mother Death said something with a throaty laugh, but whatever language she was speaking, it was not Vorago. It was no language of the Forest.

"You can't fight her, Cass!" Dumpster said.

"Pang, get ready," Casseomae said. "You've got to get the cub back inside."

Casseomae hit the roof with a heavy swipe, then sidled to her left, leading the cat farther from the doorway.

Mother Death laughed again as she closed in on Casseomae. She had no fear in her scent and seemed to be enjoying this moment of toying with her prey.

Casseomae charged, clashing with the cat with all her weight. The blow would have sent a cougar end over end, but Mother Death hardly budged. She sank her fangs into Casseomae's shoulder, teeth reaching bone.

With a surge of anger, Casseomae burst onto her hind legs, knocking the cat off her before swiping her claws against Mother Death's throat. The blow drew blood and ripped free a clump of feathery white fur.

The cat circled away, a clever fighter who would manage how many injuries she would take before she went in for the kill. But she had opened up even more space between herself and the door.

Pang nipped the cub's fingers, then ran. The child followed with Dumpster cupped in his hand. Mother Death started after them, but Casseomae feigned a charge, driving the cat back. Before she reached her, Casseomae twisted deftly and raced back through the doorway.

"Go!" she bellowed, seeing her cub waiting for her. "Run!"

The cub didn't obey. As soon as Casseomae was inside, he grabbed the door and pulled it shut. An instant later the door rocked in its frame as Mother Death threw all her weight against it. She roared in frustration.

"Come on," Casseomae said, nudging the child ahead of her. Together they hurried down the stairs toward Pang's echoing whines.

The cats huddled and spat from the corners as they passed. "All that enter the city belong to Mother Death!"

they cried. "She will have you, dears. She is coming for you!"

Casseomae could no longer hear the enormous cat tearing at the door, but she knew they were right. Mother Death would break the door apart before long, and she would have no trouble following them.

It seemed to take longer going down the stairs than it had taken to climb them, especially to Casseomae, whose wounded shoulder burned terribly. At long last, they reached the bottom.

A throaty roar echoed down the stairwell.

"She's free," Pang said, tail tucked and shaking with fright.

"Come on," Casseomae said. The four ran to the room where Casseomae had come through the window. The wolves milled about in the alley below.

"I almost wish you'd left me to those crazed pusses!" Dumpster squeaked.

Casseomae surveyed the alley. Down a little way was the metal dumpster that blocked one end. It was filled to the top with rainwater and floating debris. On the other side, the alley continued to the far end of the building, where sunlight illuminated the empty street beyond.

The cub cried out. Casseomae turned, half expecting to see the enormous cat. But the child was waving a hand at her from the hallway.

"What's he saying?" Pang asked.

"No idea," Casseomae said. She ran toward him as the cub pushed open a wide pair of doors.

Mother Death roared from the stairwell, nearly to the bottom.

The child hurried through the doors with Pang at his heels. Casseomae lunged after them. A few paces ahead was a ledge with a short section of broken stairs—the ones Casseomae had collapsed when they'd first entered the building.

Mother Death landed in the hallway as the child slammed the doors shut. Her weight cracked the doors' frame, but for the moment the doors held.

"I knew you'd come back," a voice whispered below them.

Casseomae turned to look over the edge. The room below was filled with wolves, and the black-coated Ogeema stood at their center.

CHAPTER THIRTY-THREE

Casseomae felt the platform creaking under her weight.

"Stay still," Pang yipped with tucked tail.

Mother Death hit the doors again.

"What sort of trouble have you stirred up now?" the Ogeema asked.

"You don't want to know," Dumpster squeaked.

"It would probably be best if you sent your cub down here to us," the Ogeema said. A deep-throated chorus of growls filled the room.

The cub had his back against the doors, wide eyes drifting over the army of wolves. A sudden blow from Mother Death knocked him forward. Casseomae caught his arm with her teeth and pulled him away from the edge.

"Get behind me, cub," she growled.

The child crouched against the wall with Dumpster running madly across his shoulders.

"What do we do?" Pang asked, looking from the doors to the wolves. "She'll be through those doors soon."

The next blow sent a crack down the center of one of the doors.

"If not sooner," Casseomae said. She stood on her hind legs and, struggling to ignore the seething wound in her shoulder, leaned her full weight against the doors. Mother Death hit them again with a furious howl.

"Best come down with us," the Ogeema suggested. "Let us protect you from . . . whatever it is you've disturbed."

The cat rammed the doors again, and a shard of wood broke away, slamming into Casseomae's nose. The doors were crumbling. Another blow, and Mother Death would be through.

As she listened to Mother Death circling for a final charge, Casseomae had a desperate idea. If Mother Death hit the doors expecting Casseomae to be blocking the doors with her weight . . .

Casseomae dropped to all fours and pushed Pang and the cub against the wall.

"What are you doing?" Pang yipped. The cub grasped Casseomae's paw in panic.

The doors exploded into pieces as Mother Death burst through. The cat pitched forward, her claws spread against the floor. But she was going the wrong direction for those hooks to help her. She slid down the short set of remaining stairs, her head tipping over the edge, her back legs flying up.

She could not stop herself. She fell into the wolves below.

There was a moment of utter quiet, then a swell of horrific noise. Barks and growls. Roars and howls. Sounds Casseomae had never heard coming from wolf or cat.

Pang gathered his wits first, dashing through the shattered doors. Dumpster leaped from the cub and followed, with Casseomae and the cub right behind him. The four ran to the room overlooking the alley.

Dumpster climbed into the window. "They're leaving," he said.

Casseomae stuck her head through the opening. The wolves that had been on watch were running down the alley to join the fight.

"It's still too far down to jump," Casseomae said.

Dumpster was already out the window, scampering down a ledge that ran along the face of the building. He stopped just over the dumpster at the far end of the alley.

The rat snapped his tail and leaped. He landed with a plop in the pool of rainwater filling the metal container.

Bobbing to the surface a moment later, he paddled to the side, where he climbed up on the edge and shook the water from his fur.

Pang eyed the ledge dubiously. "It's too narrow," he panted.

Casseomae peered out the window. The ledge was too narrow for Pang and certainly too narrow for her. Suddenly the cub poked his head out of a window farther down the ledge. The window was right over the dumpster.

The cub waved at her and chirped cheerfully.

"Come on, old bear," Pang said, running into the hallway.

Casseomae followed, the awful roars and howls of the battle louder inside. Pang led her to a room down the hall where the cub was climbing out the window. He squatted like a squirrel on a branch and stared down at the dumpster.

Casseomae snorted reassuringly at him. "It's safe, cub. Jump."

He took a deep breath and dropped. The child splashed into the water and came up with flailing arms. He sputtered and coughed but soon managed to climb up on the edge of the dumpster's rim. He looked up and barked for Casseomae and Pang to follow him.

"You're next," Casseomae said.

The dog ran for the window and leaped, his paws

catching the window ledge and propelling him through. Casseomae leaned out to see Pang paddling around inside the dumpster. The child slipped an arm under the dog and hoisted him onto the rim. Both dropped to the ground.

Casseomae could still hear the terrible battle being waged. They had to hurry. The fight wouldn't last forever, and then either the wolves or Mother Death would be hunting them.

She wedged herself up through the window and tumbled down. Her fall was not so well aimed, and her back hip hit the metal edge painfully. Gulping air, she hooked her claws around the dumpster's top. With a tug that sent a jolt of pain through her injured shoulder, she climbed up and over the side of the dumpster.

The cub ran up to hug her, but she nudged him away.

"I'm fine," she growled. "Pang, can you lead us from here?"

He barked and ran down the alley toward the far end. Back out in the open street, the noise of Mother Death's battle with the wolves echoed off the skyscrapers.

Pang gauged the direction of the sun through the maze of buildings around them. "This way," he said. "We just have to get to the other side of the city."

"And hope we don't encounter any more Mother Deaths," Dumpster said from the cub's shoulder.

The four ran for some time. The sun was falling

behind them when they at last left the towering sky-scrapers and reached the river once more.

"We'll follow the river, out to where it flows to the Wide Waters," Pang said. "That seems the quickest way to those spinning towers."

"The Havenlands." Casseomae nudged the cub, and he smiled his doglike smile up at her. "Just a little farther," she said. "And then you'll be safe, my cub."

CHAPTER THIRTY-FOUR

Although they were all exhausted, even the cub managed to walk until sunset. The Forest again surrounded them, the last ruins of the city's outskirts far behind. Whenever possible, they walked in the shallows to mask their scent. But much of the river's edge was clogged with rusting debris, and the water was often too deep and swift for them to safely follow.

The pain in Casseomae's hip had subsided, but her shoulder ached where Mother Death had bitten her. That night the pain repeatedly woke her. She tried to lick the wound, but it was in a spot she could not reach.

"You all right?" Pang asked her in the morning.

Casseomae took a few steps to break open an ant mound for a meal but almost immediately slumped back to the ground. "It's that cat's bite," she said.

The dog trotted over to investigate. "It looks bad."

"It's infected," Dumpster said, climbing up to take a closer look.

"It's what?" Casseomae said.

"Those cats have nasty teeth," the rat replied. "You need it cleaned, or it'll get worse."

Pang volunteered to lick at the wound. Casseomae endured it as long as she could before rising. "We've got to go."

Dumpster allowed the child to carry him. As they were walking, Casseomae said, "Those cats acted like they had seen your mischief."

"I know," the rat replied. "Sounded like they did more than just see them."

"I suppose it did," Casseomae said. "But I also got the feeling that at least some of them got away."

"Maybe," Dumpster said, resting glumly in the cub's cupped palm.

By the afternoon, the ache in Casseomae's shoulder had grown terribly. Each step on her front paw brought with it a stab of pain.

"You're limping," Pang said. "Let me clean it some more."

Casseomae grunted. She lay in a patch of cool shade while the dog licked away the dried blood and oozing pus.

"I think it's getting worse," he finally said.

"I've been bitten deeper," Casseomae said, though

in fact she had not. She lumbered over to the river to lie down in the water, letting it seep into the stinging wound.

The cub gathered hard plums from a tree and waded into the river to offer them to her.

"No, cub," Casseomae snorted. "You feed yourself. I can still forage just fine."

When the cub continued holding them out, Casseomae sighed and took a bite.

"Look!" Pang called. He had trotted down the bank a short way and stood atop a log.

Casseomae came out of the river and followed Dumpster and the cub over. Ahead, the river widened and rounded in a bend. Over the tops of the trees, Casseomae spotted the tips of metal fins rising and falling lazily.

"How far away are they?" Dumpster asked.

"Can't tell," Pang replied. "Let's keep going."

They journeyed into the late afternoon, following the ever-widening river. When they stopped to drink, they found the water strangely salty.

"That's the Wide Waters you're tasting," Pang said excitedly. "I've always heard they taste of blood. They say that unless you're a fish, you can't drink from them."

"Is it poisoned?" Dumpster asked, drawing back from the bank.

"I don't know," Pang said. "Maybe it's best we drink from the Forest's puddles from now on."

They caught more glimpses of the towers as they went, and soon even the red glowing eyes in the towers' centers.

"They're like flowers," Pang said.

"I've never seen flowers like that," Dumpster said. "Flower petals don't spin around."

"They still look like flowers," the dog said, trotting around a rusting vehicle. "To me, anyway."

"What's strange are the lights," Dumpster said. "Lights need electricity to glow. That's one of those things that disappeared with the Old Devils."

"Then how are they doing that?" Casseomae asked.

"Scratch me bald if I know," Dumpster said.

Casseomae puzzled on it, feeling slow-headed with the pain spilling from her shoulder.

When the sun had set and the Forest darkened, Pang asked, "Should we rest for the night?"

Casseomae glanced behind them. "I'd feel better sleeping in the Havenlands," she said.

"Me too," Dumpster said. "My whiskers are tingling."

Pang looked back the way they had come, flicking his ear and sniffing. When he turned back, he said, "A little farther, then."

They left the riverside, tramping through the dark Forest with the glowing eyes guiding them. The cub slogged along next to Casseomae, his hand resting on her side. He murmured something melodic and birdlike that Casseomae found soothing. With each step, the lights grew closer. Just as Casseomae felt her throbbing legs could carry her no farther, she heard Pang yelp.

"What is it?" Dumpster squeaked, clawing his way onto the child's shoulder.

The dog was sniffing at a strange-looking metal branch sticking straight up from the ground. It was tall, as tall as Casseomae when she stood on her hind legs.

"I'm not sure," Pang said. "Something stung me." He took a cautious step past the metal branch, then yelped again. Tucking his tail, he circled around behind Casseomae.

"Stay back, cub," she growled. As she approached the metal branch, she could see that it was one of many running in a straight line through the Forest in both directions. Each branch was about five paces from the next, but there was nothing between them—no wires, no rusty strings of barbs, nothing.

A strange odor hovered over the place, unlike anything she'd smelled before, and a dull hum tickled her eardrums.

Casseomae touched her nose to the closest metal branch. When nothing happened, she stretched her snout into the space between the branches. Immediately a jolt of pain rushed through her body. She stumbled back and shook her head. "What was that?"

Dumpster snapped his tail. "I can't believe it. I can't scratchin' believe it."

"What is it?" Pang said.

"The lights, and now this." Dumpster flicked his whiskers. "Electricity. It's got to be electricity!"

"How do we get past it?" Casseomae asked.

"Well, as my old da used to say," Dumpster said, "'*Every fence has a gate.*'"

"What does that mean?" she asked.

"It means we need to follow these and hope there's a passage through them."

They followed the metal branches through the Forest. Soon the trees on the other side thinned out. Casseomae saw a wide expanse of land speckled with shadowy clusters. It could have been her meadow except that it was much bigger, and the grass was too short to even whisper in the night's winds.

Dumpster was staring at the shadowy shapes spread throughout the field. "What *are* those?" he asked.

"Bushes?" Casseomae guessed. "Relics?"

Then one of the shadows moved.

Pang whined and backed up a step. Casseomae lifted her nose and sampled the air. She could smell them; they were viands of some sort.

They came upon one that was near the edge of the barrier. It stood on four legs and was big, bigger even than a bear. It was eating, tearing chunks of grass from the ground. As they approached, the creature made a low sound and lumbered away. Its white eyes glowed faintly in the starlight as it looked back at them.

"A deer?" Pang guessed. "But what a fat deer!"

"That's no deer," Dumpster said. "That's a beef. But I thought they were all wiped out by the wolves after the Old Devils vanished."

"It seems that some survived here in the Haven-lands," Casseomae said. She gazed at the fat-bellied beast. There was no way it could have survived in the Forest. She doubted it could run. And it had no horns, no means to protect itself from a hunting pack.

She felt a welling of optimism that momentarily pushed aside the pain in her shoulder. If these ancient creatures had survived here, then the Havenlands really were safe from voras.

"We've got to get across," she snorted.

"You can't," squeaked a small voice from the dark.

Dumpster spun around, sniffing furiously. "Storm-drain . . . Is that you?"

CHAPTER THIRTY-FIVE

The dry leaves behind them rustled, and a rat crept out from underneath them. He stood on his hind legs and sniffed the air. "Dumpster!" he said. "Lord Murk, bless my eyes. How did you ever find us?"

Dumpster ran to greet the rat, lowering to his belly to allow Stormdrain to nip at his ears and comb his fur with his teeth. "Are the others with you?" Dumpster asked.

"They are hiding in a log nearby," Stormdrain said, flicking his whiskers toward the dark. "What few of us are left."

Dumpster sat up. "The cats? Is it true they attacked you?"

Stormdrain wrinkled his whiskers. "Yes. We were

fool enough to think that the city was the Havenlands because of the beasts in the river. Those monsters should have feasted on us, but they didn't. They were frightened of us. Beasts of that size frightened of us! What were they, Dumpster?"

"I don't know," he said. "I've seen much that the Memory can't explain."

"If only you'd been with us. You surely would have warned us of what lay in that city." Stormdrain's whiskers drooped. "We crossed the river and searched for a spot for our new colony. The shadows had hardly lengthened before we were set upon by such a number of cats as I have never seen."

"We saw," Dumpster said. "We came through the city."

"You were fortunate to have protection," he said, eyeing Casseomae. "We ran for the river. Many were caught by the pusses or simply lost in the panic. All that are left could sleep in a single burrow. And here at last we have found the Havenlands, Murk bless us, but alas there is no way to enter. Curb, our fearless scout, died trying to cross. Something burned him alive with no fire or heat."

"It's electricity," Dumpster said.

"I thought as much, trying to conjure what you've taught me." The old rat licked at a wound on his forepaw. "I'm sorry we left you. After the skyscraper fell . . . well, we feared you were lost with the others."

"I don't blame you," Dumpster said. "You had the mischief to think of. I'm just glad to find you again."

"Me too, wise buck." The rat eyed Casseomae, Pang, and the child. "Who are your companions? And how have you charmed them into serving you?"

"Serve him!" Pang yapped. "He—"

"—has helped us enormously," Casseomae said, lowering her nose to Stormdrain.

Pang's remaining ear cocked, but he didn't argue.

Dumpster lifted his nose toward the cub. "Do you see that creature there?" Dumpster asked the old rat. "That is an Old Devil!"

Stormdrain slunk back a few steps. "What! How can this be?"

Casseomae explained how the child had fallen from the sky. "He's alone, and just a cub. He won't harm you."

"What foolishness is this!" Stormdrain squeaked. "Why would you do such a thing? You know what his kind did."

"You aren't wrong to think that," Dumpster said. "I scratchin' thought it myself. But if you had seen all that this bear has done to protect the cub, you would feel about him as I do. Besides, he's more bear and dog now than Old Devil."

Stormdrain watched Casseomae with unblinking eyes.

"We are searching for a way across this fence,"

Dumpster said. "We have to get the cub to the Havenlands and beyond. There's a safe place for him there, a place the bear can raise him without threat from the wolves. Gather the mischief. We will make our colony there."

Stormdrain sighed. "The mischief will not come. You know as well as I that as long as these voras are nearby, they will not come out, not even to greet you. It's impossible."

"Scratchin' mites, I had given up hope of ever finding you again," Dumpster said. "I can't leave you now!"

"You must," the old rat said firmly. "See if you can find this den of safety. When you do, let us know and I will try to convince the others to join you."

Dumpster flapped his tail against the ground. "Very well," he said. "Stay hidden. Keep the mischief safe. I'll return as soon as I can."

"Thank you, brave buck," Stormdrain said. The old rat rose on his hind legs to bump noses with Dumpster and then scurried into the underbrush.

As the four of them started walking again, Casseomae glanced back and saw eyes glinting in the dark. She was amazed that the rats had come so far, but then she could hardly believe she had traveled so far from her own meadow.

The wound in her shoulder was oozing again. She could feel it thickening in her fur. Just a little farther, she thought. Just a little farther and the cub would be safe.

CHAPTER THIRTY-SIX

They had walked past scores of the metal branches when Dumpster finally said, "I might have been wrong. My memory is not as scratchin' perfect as Stormdrain believes. It could be that this fence has no gate."

"What about the trees?" Pang said, looking at the ones nearest the fence. "Some of their branches hang over the fence. I can't climb, but the rest of you could try."

Casseomae looked up at the maples and dogwoods curling over the top of the fence. She feared her shoulder had lost too much strength to allow her to make the climb. Besides, the branches looked too thin to support any of them but Dumpster.

Before she could say so, Dumpster squeaked, "Don't go near it!"

Casseomae turned to see the child reaching out to touch one of the metal sticks. He chirped softly as a red square lit up on its surface.

Casseomae sniffed. Something was on the stick, something that looked like the glowing device the cub had lost in the river. The child tapped the red square, and the screen turned from red to blue. Casseomae heard a beeping sound, and the dull buzz that had been in her ears faded. The cub grinned at her before waving his hand past the metal stick.

"What's he done?" Pang asked.

"Maybe the electricity doesn't harm Old Devils," Dumpster said.

Casseomae leaned her nose forward, past the metal stick. The shock was gone. She took a step and then another until she was through the fence.

"He's opened a gate!" Dumpster squeaked.

The cub followed Casseomae into the vast meadow. Dumpster came through next, but Pang lay whimpering on the other side.

"Come on, you mangy coward!" the rat called.

With a shivering tail, Pang scooted forward and then ran full speed until he was past the others.

"We're through," Casseomae said. "Do you want to gather your mischief?"

"Let's see if it's safe first," Dumpster said.

Casseomae led them deeper into the meadow, toward

the spinning towers. Up close, they were huge, far taller than any of the skyscrapers in the city.

More of the fat beefs lowed and trudged about the meadow, along with other creatures—smaller white viands with fluffy, cloudlike coats. The beasts ignored them or moved away slowly when they approached. They did not panic and run like deer would have. Their numbers were enormous, and Casseomae could only guess it was because they were not hunted.

The air smelled different here, sharp, like nothing Casseomae had ever encountered in the Forest. They walked past the towers and over hills until the meadow grass ended at a bluff. Beyond, a silvery expanse stretched to the horizon.

"The Wide Waters," Pang said. He and the cub ran down the slope with excited barks. For Casseomae, the climb down was brutal. Waves of pain passed through her with each step.

"Cass?" Dumpster asked with an unusual note of concern.

"I'll be fine."

They stood together in the soft sand. Gentle waves washed up to their paws, and Casseomae nearly lapped at the water before remembering Pang's warning.

Pang and the cub ran back to them. "The vultures said we would have to walk over the water," Pang panted. "How are we going to do that?"

"A bridge." Casseomae searched the night waters. "I thought there would be a bridge."

"No bridge can cross that," Dumpster said.

The cub ran playfully along the edge of the surf, kicking at the white foam.

"Stay close," Casseomae said.

The wind was cool and moist, and Casseomae felt that if she lay down she could drop into sleep immediately. But she stared out. It was all such a wonder—all that water. The world was not just the Forest. There was something else. There was more. But it was a strange, mysterious "more" here at the edge of all she had ever known or imagined.

"There is nowhere to go," Casseomae said. "Were the Auspectres wrong?"

Pang shifted uncomfortably. "It's . . . it's time I told you what I asked the Auspectres." He glanced down the beach at the cub playing in the surf, then said, "My pack was being hunted. I knew we wouldn't last much longer. I went to the Auspectres and asked what I could do.

"They said to set off on my own. That if I did, I would find a Companion, the first in generations, and that he would bring about what I most deeply wanted—the war that would destroy the wolves, the war that would free my kin.

"So I left them. I abandoned my pack, and I survived. And then I saw the pup—a Companion! Here was the one the Auspectres were talking about! The Auspectres' prophecy was coming true."

Dumpster crept beneath Casseomae, listening but saying nothing.

"But now there is no bridge, no Island of the Sun, and I've realized that I didn't find the Companion, you did. He's not my Companion, he's your cub, and you have made him part of the Forest. He is not the one to bring about the war."

Pang scratched at the sandy beach. "It seems the Auspectres were wrong for both of us."

The cub ran back up the beach, chirping and waving his hands. When he reached them, he tugged on Casseomae's forepaw. Casseomae growled with the pain but didn't have the heart to nip at him.

"Ahead," Pang said suddenly. "The cub wants us to see something."

They followed the cub along the beach until a concrete structure came into view. It started on the dunes and stretched out like a highway over the water.

Casseomae and Pang looked at each other.

"Pluck my whiskers," Dumpster said. "It's a bridge!"

They climbed the dunes and stepped onto the bridge's smooth surface. The bridge was several strides wide with low walls on either side. Tall poles with spheres of glass at the top stood along the walls.

Dumpster scrambled up one of the walls. "You know

what's strange about this place?" he asked. "There aren't any relics here. No rusting vehicles. No crumbling Old Devil dens back in that meadow."

"Maybe the Skinless were never here," Casseomae said.

"They had to have been," Dumpster replied. "Who else built that electric fence, those spinning towers, or this scratchin' bridge?"

They heard a strange sound, as if all the beefs back in the meadow were lowing at once.

Casseomae looked worriedly at her friends. "I think we've just run out of time. Pang, get the cub to the island. Hurry! Dumpster, you go with them."

But Pang, the cub, and Dumpster were staring past her. Casseomae turned to see wolves streaming toward the dunes. Leading the pack was the Ogeema.

CHAPTER THIRTY-SEVEN

"Let's go!" Dumpster cried, scurrying up the child's leg.

Pang led the way down the bridge at a run, the cub sprinting after him. Casseomae brought up the rear, her forepaws pounding on the bridge's hard surface, each step a searing pain in her shoulder.

They ran blindly into the darkness, trusting that the bridge led somewhere. Dumpster perched on the cub's shoulder. Clinging to the cub's ear, he peered past Casseomae at the pursuing wolves.

"They're just on the bridge," Dumpster said. "There are a lot of them, but not as many as there were before. That cat has left them scratchin' battled and bruised. Half are limping."

Casseomae glanced over her shoulder. Dumpster was

right. There were fewer than before, but there were still too many, especially with her shoulder the way it was.

And the wolves were gaining on them.

Casseomae swung back around. Her cub was at Pang's side, keeping a furious pace. He was so tough now, so brave, no longer the small, scared thing she had rescued from the coyotes. She was proud of him and knew that if he could only make it to the island, he would survive.

Behind her, Casseomae heard the panting and growling of the wolves as they closed the distance between them. The next moment, she felt teeth latch on to her side. She roared and twisted, freeing herself from the wolf's jaws. The cub looked back at her, and his eyes widened in fear. His feet tangled, and he fell hard, catching himself with his open palms.

Casseomae pivoted on her hind legs and swiped a forepaw through the air, slamming the leading wolf to the ground. She lunged to the other side and closed her jaws around the throat of the next, then hurled it into the pack. She locked her legs and popped open her jaws, roaring death at the wolves now skidding to a halt.

The pack were fewer but still easily filled the width of the bridge. They growled at her, showing her teeth and flattened ears. Behind her, Casseomae could hear the cub choking back sobs as Pang urged him to his feet. Run, she thought. Run!

The pack shifted, and suddenly the Ogeema was standing before her.

"Old bear," whispered the enormous black wolf. He stared at her with one icy blue eye. The other was closed, that side of his face torn by three fresh gashes from Mother Death. "The Skinless One must die. You know this."

"He is no longer one of the Skinless, Ogeema," Casseomae said. "He is my cub. He understands and respects the Forest. He is no threat to it, or to you."

Behind her, Casseomae could hear Pang whining and the cub's short, angry chirps. What were they doing? Why weren't they running?

The Ogeema pulled back his lips in a quiet laugh. "I have crossed great distances and subjugated pack after pack to end this threat. I will not return while it continues to breathe."

Casseomae felt quick claws climbing her hind leg and hurrying across her back. "The cub won't leave you!" Dumpster whispered into her ear. "Pang has tried, but the cub refuses to go!"

Casseomae's heart dropped. Despite her wound, she would kill every wolf here, including the Ogeema. But in the chaos of the fight, only one or two wolves would need to get by her for all to be lost.

She would not let it happen. She raked her claw

against the smooth surface of the bridge and roared her fury at the Ogeema and his army.

The Ogeema lifted his ears in surprise and then slowly began backing into the pack. "Very well, old bear," he whispered. His wolves closed around him and advanced, all teeth and snarls.

Suddenly the globes at the top of the posts all along the bridge erupted in brilliant light. Casseomae shut her eyes against the glare and roared, snapping her jaws blindly, but the wolves didn't seem to be attacking. They were just as confused as she was.

Still, she had to know what was going on. Casseomae blinked her eyes open and saw the Ogeema standing in the midst of his frenzied pack. He was staring past her, his ears flat against his head.

"No," he whispered. "It cannot be!"

Casseomae turned to look.

Silhouetted against the light were several creatures that looked like the cub, but taller.

Skinless Ones.

For all the cub had changed her, Casseomae felt a sudden terror at the appearance of these creatures from myth, these destroyers of the Forest and its tribes. They wore devices on their faces and carried metal sticks in their hands like the one the cub had found.

They raised the sticks and pointed them at the wall of wolves.

Fire flashed. Thunder roared.

Something stung Casseomae's hip, and she slumped to the ground. Behind her the wolves screamed as the Skinless fire and noise cut into them. In moments the entire pack lay spread over the bridge in twisted, tormented positions.

The Ogeema lay in blood, his blue eye open and his tongue hanging out.

Casseomae heard her cub cry out and felt his little body as he threw himself against her, sinking his face and hands into her fur.

"It's all right, cub," she said. She licked at his ears, nuzzling her wet nose against him, then climbed painfully to her feet.

The Skinless began shouting, not the chirping noises her cub used but deeper, louder bellows. They pointed their sticks at her and called to the cub.

Then a different voice rang out. It was not the deep bellow of these killers or the chirp of her cub. This voice was softer and yet full of authority.

This new Skinless stepped in front of the others. It was a she, though Casseomae wasn't sure how she knew that. She did not wear the devices of the others, and she did not carry a storm-bringing stick. She wore a simple blue clothing-hide. The tuft of fur atop her head was long and meadow-grass yellow like the cub's.

She spread her arms and called gently to the cub.

Then she said something to the other Skinless, and one by one they lowered their weapons. She looked to the side of the bridge, where Pang stood trembling in fear. She knelt and held a hand out to him, smiling. Pang tucked his tail and approached to sniff her fingers. He got close enough for her to pat his ears, then slipped away to stand with Casseomae and the cub.

"I think she wants to help the pup," Pang said softly.

Casseomae felt Dumpster's claws as he shifted his perch to peer around her. "Why doesn't he go to her, then?" he said.

The child clung to Casseomae's neck. Casseomae licked him again, drawing her tongue across his face, tasting the salt on his skin and the dust of the Forest. "Because he's my cub," she said.

"They'll never let you take him," Dumpster squeaked, digging his claws into her. "They'll kill you. They'll kill us all."

The woman called out. She was still kneeling, and her eyes were wet.

The cub relaxed his hold on Casseomae but did not turn.

"You're not like them," Casseomae breathed into the cub's ear. "You're one of us. One of the Forest."

But with a sting in her breast, she realized this wasn't true. While the cub knew something of the Forest, he would never truly have a place there—the other vora would never trust him, and the wolves would always hunt him.

Casseomae had set out to find a safe place for him, and that place was here.

The woman spoke gently, and the child trembled. His blue eyes stared straight into Casseomae's. Casseomae grunted, rubbing her snout against the cub. She nipped gently at his arm. "Go to her."

The cub took a step back, then pressed his nose against Casseomae's. "It's safe," he snorted softly.

Casseomae sat back on her haunches, transfixed. He had spoken. There was no mistaking it. He had spoken to her in Vorago!

The cub backed away, then turned and ran to the woman. She gathered him in her arms and swung him around, pressing her mouth to him over and over.

When she let him go, the cub was grinning. He looked to Pang, and the dog dashed over to him in a flash.

"How did I know that stupid cur was going to stay with them?" Dumpster said.

"He's found his Companions," Casseomae said simply.

The woman looked at Casseomae. She spoke briefly to the other Skinless before turning and carrying the child away in her arms. Pang glanced happily back at them before following her.

The cub watched Casseomae over the woman's

shoulder, his blue eyes as big and wide as the sky. Then he disappeared into the blinding glare of the bridge lights. The remaining Skinless lowered their weapons and followed.

Casseomae and Dumpster sat in silence and watched them go. After a time, the lights clicked off, and Casseomae and Dumpster were left in darkness. But as her eyes adjusted, Casseomae saw that dawn was beginning to break in the direction that the child had gone. The sky at the end of the bridge was getting lighter.

Casseomae turned and began making her way through the bodies of the wolves strewn across the ground. She crossed from the bridge to the dunes and, both her shoulder and hip stinging, climbed to the top.

"Look!" Dumpster squeaked.

Five coyotes were standing in the meadow. Rend and her rout. Overhead in the gray morning sky, vultures circled on long black wings. The Auspectres had arrived to collect their due.

"They all smell death," Casseomae said. "Let's find your mischief, Dumpster. Let's leave this place."

Casseomae cast one last look back. The bridge seemed to stretch out to where the red sun was rising from the Wide Waters. And in the glow, Casseomae could just make out an island with buildings and passerings.

"Do you think the cub's tribe has returned to this

island from the sky?" Casseomae asked. "Or do you reckon they were here all along?"

"Scratch if I know." Dumpster clicked his teeth. "There's no Memory to answer that."

Dumpster jumped down and ran ahead, eager to reach his mischief. Casseomae limped slowly, nursing her injuries. As she came down from the dunes, Rend and her rout loped away, disappearing into the tree line.

Casseomae made her way across the meadow and through the metal sticks of the fence. Dumpster and a scattering of rats were just ahead, in the low brush next to a rotten log. As Casseomae started toward them, she heard a pulse of sound. The Skinless fence had come back to life, and once again, the Havenlands were closed.

"However they've come," she said, thinking not of her cub but of the other Skinless and their weapons, "let's just hope they stay. Let's just hope they don't want the Forest again."

CHAPTER THIRTY-EIGHT

That winter the snow came hard, which made for a wet spring. Casseomae's meadow was thick with wildflowers and delicious insects. Nesting birds darted through the shattered windows of vine-tangled relics to bring food to their hatchlings.

A yearling cub rolled at Casseomae's feet. He growled and nipped at her chin. His fur was fuzzy and full of leaves. Casseomae pushed him with her snout, saying, "Get on, you little rascal."

He ignored her, climbing onto Casseomae's back. Her shoulder still ached dully from Mother Death's bite, but the infection had long since healed, as had the wound in her hip.

"You've gotten too big for that," Casseomae growled, rolling onto her side to throw the cub off.

Dubhe came around a relic, her other two cubs beside her. They had grown bigger over the winter. By fall they would be on their own. The cubs stared at Casseomae with their usual mixture of fear and respect.

"There he is," Dubhe said. "Casseomae, I hope he hasn't been bothering you again."

"No," she snorted. "He's fine. A strong little one you've got there. He reminds me of Chief Alioth when he was a cub. Maybe he'll be chief one day."

"Maybe," Dubhe said. "If he does, his rule will be peaceful, thanks to you." She gathered her cub and set off to forage in the Forest.

Casseomae stretched in her den's doorway, enjoying the warm sun. She had hardly closed her eyes before clicking teeth woke her. Casseomae grunted. "It seems the sloth hears strange new stories every day of what I did."

Dumpster wiggled his whiskers. "I don't scratchin' know what you're talking about," he said. "You think my mischief talks to bears? Not likely!"

"Then why do they think I rid the Forest of the Ogeema and his pack?" Casseomae asked.

"Must be the coyotes," Dumpster said. "Those underlickin' sons of curs are trying to stir up the packs again."

Casseomae snorted dubiously. "More likely some rodents are hoping to keep voras out of my meadow and away from their colony."

"Delusional, old bear," the rat said, scampering back into the thick grass. "Completely delusional, you are."

Casseomae closed her eyes and settled back in the sunshine. She had just drifted to sleep again when another sound woke her. She lifted her head. The sound was familiar, but it filled her with unease. It sounded like a distant roar, and it came from the sky.

She looked up as the roar grew and then changed to a whoosh of wind, quickly growing quieter and receding into the distance. She saw the source of the sound before it disappeared over the treetops. It was black and birdlike in shape. But it was no bird.

In a moment, it was gone.

Slowly, the familiar sounds of the Forest returned. Casseomae looked once more to the sky before lumbering into her den.

ACKNOWLEDGMENTS

J. R. R. Tolkien said that story ideas arise from "the leaf-mould of the mind." This story grew out of the rich compost of Alan Weisman's speculative science book *The World Without Us*; Native American creation myths; one of the first postapocalyptic novels (and possibly the only hopeful one), *Earth Abides* by George R. Stewart; and the animal-fantasy classics *The Jungle Book* by Rudyard Kipling and *Watership Down* by Richard Adams.

Stories don't just fall from the sky, and *The Prince Who Fell from the Sky* would not have come about without the insights and help of many wonderful and talented people. To those friends and colleagues—many of whom could not be named here—I am eternally grateful.

Thanks to my editor, Jim Thomas, whose brilliant instincts and creative vision deepened the characters and brought out the heart of this story. Also thanks to Lauren Donovan, Chelsea Eberly, Sarah Nasif, and the other wonderful people at Random House Children's Books.

To my agent, Josh Adams, for his persistence and unwavering enthusiasm. Your talents are manifold, not least of them being your ability to always help push my stories in the best direction.

To my critique group, Jennifer Harrod, Stephen Messer, and Jen Wichman (aka J. J. Johnson). Your guidance as writers and caring as friends have allowed me to take artistic risks I never would have ventured without your thoughtful and honest suggestions.

A final special thanks to my wife, Amy Gorely. Your love and support have helped keep all things in balance.

JOHN CLAUDE BEMIS is the author of the fantasy-steampunk trilogy the Clockwork Dark, which is composed of *The Nine Pound Hammer, The Wolf Tree,* and *The White City.* His books have been described as "original and fresh" and "a unique way of creating fantasy." John lives with his wife and daughter in Hillsborough, North Carolina.